KT-362-479

First published in 2019 by Gomer Press,
Llandysul, Ceredigion SA44 4JL
www.gomer.co.uk

ISBN: 978 1 78562 309 7

A CIP record for this title is available from the British Library.

This book is published with the financial support of the
Books Council of Wales.

Printed and bound in Wales at
Gomer Press, Llandysul, Ceredigion

THE NIGHTMARE GIFT

GRAHAM HOWELLS

Gomer

I t was a bright autumn morning, and in a pleasant wooded valley in West Wales, a small stream babbled and crows cawed lazily. Nestled amongst the trees that shimmered gold and orange, there was a quiet village stirring at the start of a new day.

Just like any other day, children were making their way towards the village school, and in the playground they gathered and played.

For one boy entering the school, though, this was not like any other day. His name was Aled, and he was a worrier. For as long as he could remember Aled had been frightened of almost everything, and today he was especially anxious because this was the start of Aled's first day in a new school. Aled's parents had returned to Wales after working abroad, and now here he was, in a strange place surrounded by strangers.

Aled stopped in the doorway of the school. 'Please new school, please be kind to me. Help me not to be afraid in this new place.' And nervously he entered.

Mr Jenkins, the headteacher, was standing at the front of the classroom looking at the children sitting quietly in front of him.

'Today, class, we have a new boy with us. Stand up, Aled.' Aled did as he was told and went bright red as all eyes turned on him.

'I'm sure you'll make lots of new friends here, Aled. We're a friendly bunch. You can sit down now,' said Mr Jenkins smiling. 'Also, Mrs Davies won't be in today children.'

'Awww,' moaned the children playfully.

'I know, I know, but instead Miss Ceridwen will be with you.' Then Miss Ceridwen stepped forward.

Aled stared at his new teacher. He had the feeling that there was something definitely odd about Miss Ceridwen. She had flowers in her hair, and her clothes were a bit strange too, but there was something else that Aled couldn't quite work out.

'Thank you, Mr Jenkins,' she said in a voice that sounded like a warm breeze on summer leaves. 'Good morning to you class.'

'Gooood moooorning, Miiisss Ceriiidwen,' droned the children in their singsong way.

'I'll leave you to it then,' said Mr. Jenkins as he left the classroom.

'Today Mrs Davies wanted to talk to you about Halloween,' said Miss Ceridwen.

Oh no, thought Aled, Halloween was his absolutely least favourite time of the year as it was the most scary.

Miss Ceridwen started to move slowly around

the classroom, so smoothly that it seemed as if she floated.

'As you know, class, this part of West Wales is full of magical stories.'

She stopped moving and looked intently into every young face in the room. Then she looked at Aled and she smiled a little. Aled went red again and had to look away to avoid those piercing blue eyes.

'Indeed,' she continued, 'the caves and crevices of this very valley have been home to every kind of magical creature. Isn't that exciting children?'

What was she going on about? thought Aled. She sounded like she believed this stuff. He looked around the classroom and saw that everyone was transfixed by Miss Ceridwen.

'So, I want you to write a story about the magic in your valley at this special time of year; a fabulous Halloween story,' she said.

Aled groaned to himself. Not a fairy story!

Suddenly Miss Ceridwen was standing beside Aled's desk, her deep blue eyes staring down at him. Aled went red and gulped.

'You have a problem with the task, Aled.' It wasn't a question.

'Um …' said Aled. Was she reading his mind?

'Yes, Aled?' said Miss Ceridwen waiting.

'It's just that … these stories … they're not … they're not real, Miss. Isn't it a waste of time writing stories about made up things?' He clapped his hand to his mouth, and the class around him gasped. What had made him say that? It was what he was thinking, but he hadn't meant to say it out loud!

Aled hunched his shoulders and closed his eyes tight shut, bracing himself for the telling off, when Miss Ceridwen started to laugh, and the lovely sound of it filled the classroom.

'You really shouldn't believe everything you think, Aled,' said Miss Ceridwen chuckling.

'Never mind, you shall discover that magic is in the bones of your new home.' Then, from a pouch that hung from her belt she took a strange little envelope and handed it to Aled. The odd brown paper and wax seal made it look like something from a museum – very old and delicate.

'Could you take this to the nice little man in the

storeroom over there?' she asked. 'He was a new boy himself a little while ago, and he'll be able to help you with your story.' Miss Ceridwen indicated the door in the corner of the classroom.

'In the storeroom, Miss? A little man?' asked Aled very puzzled. This must be some sort of joke, he thought.

Aled looked at the door. He'd seen Mr. Jenkins open it earlier while the class was getting seated, and in it was just a very small room that was empty apart from the shelves of paints, paintbrushes, and files.

Aled looked at Miss Ceridwen, and then he got up and walked over to the storeroom.

'There's a little man in the storeroom, Miss?' he asked disbelieving. No one else in the classroom seemed to notice what was going on.

'Yes, Aled,' said Miss Ceridwen. She turned back to the class. 'So, class, while Aled gets his story going, are we all looking forward to the school trip tomorr ... '

Aled didn't hear what Miss Ceridwen said next because he had opened the storeroom door, but inside there was no storeroom. Instead, where there should have been shelves and paintbrushes there was a large, very dark, very old fashioned room.

Unusually for him, Aled was more fascinated than scared, and he took a step inside, and he saw that he was in the main room of an old cottage. As his eyes adjusted to the gloom he noticed that in the middle of the room was a long, dark wooden table. On the table were clay jugs, wooden bowls, and an unlit candle. Beyond the table was an ancient grandfather clock standing against the wall.

The room was warm and the smell of wood smoke came from a large fireplace where logs were burning. There was a small window in the corner of the room but the view out of it was not of a place outside the school.

Everything about the cottage felt ancient, but at the same time it looked as good as new, and Aled was amazed.

'Hello,' said a small voice from nearby.

'WAAAAAH!!' screamed Aled, nearly jumping out of his skin. Sitting on a small wooden stool next to the fire, and poking it with a stick, was a very small man with pointy ears and a pointy hat. Around his

waist he seemed to be wearing a ragged skirt held up with a piece of old rope.

Aled turned around to go back through the storeroom door, but it was now an old wooden cottage door that was closed and wouldn't open!

'Welcome to this Bwbach's humble home,' said the Bwbach bowing low. 'You're not leaving already?' he asked cheerily, stepping into the middle of the room. 'Don't you have a message for me?'

Aled stood with his back against the door, staring down wide-eyed.

'Message? Um … Oh … You mean the envelope?'

'Probably,' said the Bwbach holding out his hand.

'How did you know about it?' Aled asked, handing over the strange envelope that Miss Ceridwen had given him. It was then that he noticed, written across it in an ornate script:

'For The Attention Of The Bwbach'

'A little bird told me,' said the Bwbach pointing to a little bird outside the window. The Bwbach opened the wax seal on the envelope and took out a note that he read by the light of the crackling fire.

'Woohoo! Lady Ceridwen says you're a new boy!'

said the Bwbach. Aled, with panic starting to grow, stared in confusion at the strange little man.

'I didn't know anyone either when my cottage and I got here,' said the Bwbach happily. Aled, shaking now, didn't have a clue what the little man was talking about, and just stood there. 'Lady Ceridwen says that on this special day what you need is a bit of company.'

'Special day? Company? I need to get back to the classroom,' said Aled in a weak, desperate voice. 'Please let me go back,' he begged.

'You're right,' said the Bwbach. 'There's no time to waste.' And the Bwbach turned and walked over to an old wooden dresser, full of cupboards and drawers.

'You will have to be very quiet for a second, it's a bit nervous around strangers.' The Bwbach knocked a complicated knock on one of the cupboards in the dresser.

Nothing stirred, and Aled, trembling, just stared at the little Bwbach smiling back at him. Then suddenly …

'RAAAAAAAAAAAAAAAAAR!'

Something horrifying and hairy exploded from out of the cupboard and into the room. Aled yelled and crouched down into a corner. With his eyes tight shut behind his hands, Aled listened horror-struck as something banged and roared around the cottage.

'Oh yes,' shouted the Bwbach over the racket, 'perhaps I should have mentioned he can be a bit excitable!'

Aled cautiously took his hands away from his face and opened his eyes.

'Wha … wha … what is it?' Aled demanded, terrified. Something hideous with terrible yellow eyes was bouncing in front of him and changing shape and size as it did. Aled huddled tight in the corner, watching in horrified fascination as the thing became a giant spider, a mop, a fat toad, a spoon ... and on it went, constantly changing shape.

'It's a Bwci Bo,' explained the Bwbach, 'though it's true they can be hard to recognise when shapeshifting. It's been staying with me for a while as it's between homes at the moment. It'll be nice for it to get out and stretch its legs … or its tentacles … or whatever.'

The Bwbach held up the message from Miss Ceridwen for the fidgety Bwci Bo to read. Holding its shape as a hairy little dragon the creature looked at the note, then looked at Aled.

'Do take care of him won't you. He can be very sensitive,' explained the Bwbach as he patted the panting little dragon.

'I'm not looking after anything!' protested Aled. 'Just let me go back!'

'Good thinking. Lady Ceridwen will be waiting.'

Aled fumbled with the door latch, and now it opened.

He jumped through the door and found himself back in the classroom. He was shaking from head to toe standing by the storeroom door, and then he noticed that the other children were leaving the classroom. He turned to Miss Ceridwen.

'Everything okay, Aled?' she enquired as she shuffled papers on the desk. 'You look a little shaken.'

'Bwci ... Bwci ... Bwci ...' stammered Aled.

'Never mind that now, Aled. It's home time.'

'Home ... home time? I wasn't in there for that long!'

'Yes, time flies when you're having fun,' said Miss Ceridwen. 'See you tomorrow on the trip. Enjoy yourself tonight.'

'Fun? That wasn't fun ... what? What's happening tonight?'

Laughing to herself, Miss Ceridwen was already gliding out of the classroom leaving Aled alone, shocked and shaking.

Aled grabbed his rucksack; he needed to get out of this mad school as quickly as he could.

'Whoa! Whoa! Hold on there, what's the hurry?' A big ginger-haired boy appeared from the corridor and blocked Aled's way out of the classroom. 'You're new here and I've got to explain the special Halloween rules. If I see you out trick-or-treating tonight you've got to give me all your chocolate, okay?'

Oh no, thought Aled, on top of everything else there's a school bully.

Aled had no intention of going trick-or-treating, so readily said, 'Will do!' and squeezed past the boy and hurried away.

Aled's Mamgu was waiting for him outside the school and he ran to her. He always felt safe around Mamgu. Her bright, whacky, home-made clothes, and constant cheeriness settled his worries. Aled's parents were in work and wouldn't be home yet, so Aled and his Mamgu started off towards her house on the edge of the village.

'So how was the first day then? It's Halloween today, did you do anything spooky?' she asked.

'Yes … Yes, I did,' said Aled.

'Great, you'll have to tell me all about it … hey, who's this?' she said looking down.

Aled looked too, and saw that following them was the ugliest, scruffiest little dog Aled had ever seen.

'Isn't he lovely!' Mamgu declared picking up the creature. 'I haven't seen him around here before, and he's got no collar.'

Oh dear, thought Aled, Mamgu loved any stray

creature. She was always looking after them, which meant this little scruffbag was coming home with them. It was then that Aled noticed the creature's terrible yellow eyes. They would fill his nightmares forever because they were the eyes of a monster!

'Aww, he looks so hungry,' cooed Mamgu.

'He'll eat your face off, Mamgu!'

'Oh, you are funny, Aled.'

'It's … it's the … Bwci Bo,' stammered Aled in horror.

'Good name. We'll call him Bwci Bo,' said Mamgu, and she cuddled the horrendous little beast all the way home.

In Mamgu's kitchen Aled stared in terror as the Bwci Bo gobbled up a giant bowl of rice pudding and chopped bananas that she'd put down for it.

'You should take fluffy little Bwci Bo out for a walk, Aled, before it gets too dark.'

'Wha …?' And before he had time to protest Mamgu had found a lead and a collar, happily fastened the collar around the monster's neck, put the lead into Aled's hand, and ushered boy and beast out the front door.

Outside Aled stood there looking down at the Bwci Bo. He was taking a *monster* for a walk! But he was wrong; the creature was taking *him* for a *run*! It shot off away from the house, dragging Aled behind it whimpering. Aled tried to let go of the lead but somehow he couldn't open his hand.

'Stop! Stop!' he yelled, but he knew it was useless, and on they ran.

Along the road they ran, down lanes, and then onto small stony paths that led off towards the woods. Now Aled was seriously concerned; he hadn't been in the village very long and soon they were in a part of the woods that Aled didn't recognise.

They seemed to have run a long way, racing through the clawed branches that pulled at Aled's school uniform, when the Bwci Bo came to a sudden stop. Aled skidded, nearly bumping into the little creature.

It was getting dark now, but Aled could make out that they were in a clearing in the woods where everything was covered in soft, green moss. In the middle of the clearing was a small, rocky hill with two small trees growing from the top of it.

The air was very still here and a mist was starting to rise.

As he stood there with his legs wobbling, too worn out to move, Aled realised that he was now lost in creepy woods with a hideous monster, and he had never felt so terrified in all his life.

A shiver went through Aled. Then the air started to crackle, and around the small hill with its two trees a strange light started to dance in the mist.

With a deep, rocky rumble, the hill started to grow. It rose up, and as it did, within the gnarly roots of its two trees, two large round eyes slowly opened. They were pale, yellow, ancient eyes. They glowed, and Aled saw they were looking straight at him.

Then Aled got even more terrified. Next to him the Bwci Bo let out a sudden, shrill, blood-curdling howl and Aled nearly fainted from the shock of it.

'Greetings to you, too, Bwci Bo. Ha! ... Ha ha!' rumbled The Hill, amused. 'A fearful boy and a Bwci Bo have come to visit Old Hill on Hallow's Eve. Ha!' he said in a voice as deep and hollow as the deepest cave.

Aled had the mind-boggling thought that he

needed to explain himself to a hill: 'The Bwci Bo dragged me here! I don't know why!' he blurted.

Aled looked at the Bwci Bo sitting next to him on the other end of the lead. As he watched, the collar around its neck snapped and the Bwci Bo took the form of a small, hairy dragon; one of its favourite shapes? Aled wondered, distracted for a moment. 'And I'm having a really, really strange and scary day,' he said, remembering where he was.

'Ha ha!' boomed The Hill. 'ONLY WHEN IT IS DARK DO YOU KNOW HOW BRAVE YOU ARE!'

A rumble deep underground felt like laughter and Aled started to feel a strange, tickling feeling rising up his legs. He looked down to see points of light swirling up from the mossy ground around his feet. There was a loud 'Whoosh!' and Aled's ears popped. Something had changed.

Aled looked up at The Hill suddenly realising that he was feeling something he'd never experienced before; he was feeling almost *calm*. The dread in him had now been replaced with a kind of stillness. Had he gone right through terror and come out the other side? Aled wondered.

'I'm not brave at all,' said Aled. 'But I don't think I'm afraid right now. Does that mean you've magicked my fear away?'

'Not at all,' said The Hill. 'For the moment you have stopped believing everything that you think. Very wise.'

'Umm …?' said Aled, not knowing what that meant.

'On Hallow's Eve the veil between the magic and the mortal world is thin and two worlds join to celebrate the Unseen. Your meeting with the noble Bwbach, and everything that follows from it, is a rare Halloween gift from Lady Ceridwen,' rumbled The Hill.

'How? Why? What sort of gift is it; is it a nasty gift?' asked Aled.

'HA! HO!' The Hill laughed. 'Faerie magic has little to do with "How?", "Why?" and "What?"'

'But the Bwci Bo must have brought me here for a reason?' Aled enquired hopefully.

'Possibly. Though that sounds very much like a "Why?" question.'

'Am I here to get superpowers?' asked Aled hopefully.

'No,' said The Hill flatly.

 28

'Oh. Am I here to get something from you?' asked Aled. 'Something good, not horrible?' he added hastily.

'If you like.' The Hill shrugged, as much as any hill could shrug. 'How about I give to you ten leaves of ivy, but it is vital that you be the one to pick them. Throw one of the ten away, and then grind the remaining nine leaves into powder. When placed under your pillow before sleep the ground ivy shall grant you the power to see hags!'

'Errrm … could I say "No thank you" to that?' asked Aled awkwardly. 'I can't see that coming in useful any time soon.'

'Really? Hmm, okay then,' The Hill pondered, looking at Aled intently. 'This shall be my gift to a Mighty Worrier on Hallow's Eve:

You worried about the Past when it is a place never to be revisited. You agonised over the Future, which is an ever-changing place never reached. In between is Now which is where you always are. Take care of Now, and Past and Future take care of themselves.'

Something about the advice made Aled shiver, and he thought he understood.

There was a sudden yelping yap from his side that made Aled jump, and he remembered the hairy dragon Bwci Bo next to him.

'Time for the boy and Bwci Bo to join the Wild Hunt!' announced The Hill, 'HA HA! Ha Ha Ha!' and with that its glowing eyes closed, and The Hill grew smaller. *'Remember; don't believe everything you think!'* it called. 'Ha Ha Haaaaa!' The rumbling laugh faded, and the clearing was silence and mist once more.

The Bwci Bo's yelping yap started up again, and was now sounding urgent. Aled stared at the creature, and as he did the Bwci Bo transformed into a large, fierce-looking, ostrich dragon thing, all sinew and muscle. Aled gulped.

'Rrrride,' growled the ostrich dragon Bwci Bo.

'You can talk?' Aled exclaimed in amazement.

The Bwci Bo lowered itself, indicating that Aled should climb on its back. 'What? I've got to get on?' The look in the Bwci Bo's terrible face made Aled do just that.

Straight away the powerful beast bounded off through the woods. Aled held tight to the creature's bristly feathers, bending low to its back to avoid

branches, and gasping as the trees whizzed past in a blur.

Before long they were out in the open. A full moon had risen and by its light Aled could see fields he recognised. Onwards the Bwci Bo hurried until it came to a stop near Mamgu's house. Aled jumped down off its back and the Bwci Bo returned to the shape of the scruffy little dog once more.

The evening was quiet and a mist swirled lazily around their feet.

'You were in a hurry to get back here,' Aled said to the Bwci Bo. 'And what was that about a Wild Hunt?' He realised then that his parents would be home by now. They and Mamgu would be worried about him. 'Anyway, I've got to go home,' he said.

'Oi!' someone shouted, and Aled looked around to see the bully coming towards him, dressed in a black bin bag that seemed to be his Halloween costume. Was he dressed as an evil prune? Aled wondered.

'Where's my chocolate?' demanded the boy.

'Chocolate?'

'Yeah, you and your weird little dog have been out

trick-or-treating and you owe me chocolate.' Aled heard a growl next to him. Oh dear, he thought.

'I wouldn't call him weird if I were you,' advised Aled.

'Oh yeah?' said the bully surprised that Aled appeared to be standing up for himself. 'And what are you going to do about it?' he asked, looking a little less sure of things.

'Well …' said Aled.

'Baaaaad boy,' growled the Bwci Bo.

'Hey! Did …did your dog just speak?' stuttered the bully nervously.

This was when the Bwci Bo transformed itself into something truly horrendous. It shot up and sprouted claws, horns, and scales. A great, gaping mouth opened to reveal sharp, dripping fangs. Suddenly the Bwci Bo was huge and spiky, and very, very angry.

The bully stared up at the hideous monster, petrified and gibbering. The Bwci Bo monster lowered its horned head until its terrible face was level with the boy's, and then, inches away from him and eye-to-eye, the Bwci Bo let out a long, terrible, bone-chilling shrieeeeeeeek!

As the Bwci Bo screamed, monster slime sprayed from its mouth into the bully's face, and the bully, uncontrollably, screamed back at the top of his lungs.

The bully stood there with his eyes clamped shut, and screamed for quite a while. When he stopped he opened his eyes to see Aled and his scruffy dog calmly watching him, and the dog seemed to be sniggering.

'You were asking about chocolate?' said Aled hurriedly, trying to ease the uncomfortable situation. 'No, sorry, I haven't got any at the moment,' he explained. The bully gaped back with monster slime dripping down his face. 'I'm Aled, by the way. I didn't get your name?'

'Ethan,' said the slimy boy faintly, staring straight ahead wide-eyed.

'If I get some chocolate you'll be the first to know, Ethan. It's something to look forward to, hey? Lovely chocolate. Okay ...' Aled said smiling a friendly, apologetic smile. 'See ya then ...' He gave an awkward wave, and then he and the Bwci Bo turned towards Mamgu's.

They stopped outside the house; Aled crouched down to the Bwci Bo and scratched the creature under his chin. 'I have to go home now, but thanks for everything, Bo.' Bwci Bo shot out a long, prickly tongue and licked Aled's face.

Aled stood up and looked through Mamgu's window. He stood there for several minutes, not believing what he was seeing. Inside the house, as he expected, were his parents and Mamgu, and they were chatting quite happily. What shocked Aled was the thing that was sitting on the sofa. It had pointed ears, a long nose, it was two feet tall, and it was wearing Aled's clothes! When the long nosed creature noticed Aled looking in, it gave him a cheerful wave.

'WHAT?' exclaimed Aled, and he looked down at Bwci Bo. 'More faerie magic? That *thing* is pretending to be *me* isn't it! Why is THAT?'

'TRICK OR TREAT!' The shout startled Aled. He turned to see a woman floating above his Mamgu's doorstep; her old fashioned gown billowed in a leisurely way around her, and her skin was as white as her dress. She was smiling at him expectantly.

Aled looked at Bwci Bo. 'Seriously? A ghost? You've got nothing to say about this?'

'I am The White Lady,' she whispered.

'Yes, of course you are,' said Aled. By now, he thought, he really must have gone through fear and out the other side. He felt that nothing could surprise him anymore … but he was wrong.

Aled looked up into the starry sky. Overhead he thought he could make out the distant sound of many dogs barking. It was faint at first, but it grew louder, until it seemed that a pack of dogs must be gathered on Mamgu's roof.

'TRICK OR TREEEEAT!' came the sudden ghastly

screech from above. Aled had the fright of his life, which was quite a thing considering the day he was having. Suddenly a dreadful face appeared over the guttering above.

'WAAAH!' exclaimed Aled.

The face was as craggy and creased as a rotten apple, and belonged to an old crone who was grinning down at him horribly. Then she cackled an awful laugh that revealed two crooked teeth in a large gummy mouth. Somewhere behind her on the roof dogs were yapping.

Aled stepped back to the road outside Mamgu's house to get a better view of what was going on up on the roof. The White Lady floated beside him, also wanting a better look.

The full moon was high now, and it shone down on a scene that sent a chill down Aled's spine. The White Lady stood next to him smiling. There were dogs up there, but they weren't standing on the roof, they were hovering restlessly above it. They were like no dogs Aled had ever seen before, and there were lots of them.

They were large and powerful, with fur that was pure white. The inside of all their ears was red, but for Aled the most terrible thing about them was their eyes. Their eyes blazed as if on fire.

Then Aled noticed the figure in the chariot, the splendid chariot that was drawn by a beast that looked part horse, and part dragon.

The chariot rider's noble face seemed to be made up mostly of flowing, leafy green beard, and from his head grew two great antlers.

'Happy Hallow's Eve, Aled,' said the figure in a voice as deep as tree roots.

'Behold the splendour of Gwyn ap Nudd,' squeaked the wrinkled crone gesturing to the figure in the chariot. 'OLDER THAN ROCKS AND FRIEND OF THE FIRST TREES, HE IS THE GREEN KING, LORD OF ANNWN, MASTER OF THE WILD HUNT! Bow down and tremble, mortal child!' she screeched, flailing her wrinkly arms around dramatically.

'Calm down, Mallt,' said the Green King as he watched her climb down from the roof. 'There is no need for bowing or trembling,' assured the Green King as his chariot descended to land in the road. 'Aled, you shall be joining us on the Hunt.'

'What?' exclaimed Aled.

'The White Lady is here,' continued the Green King, 'and Mallt of the Night, The Hounds of Annwn, the Bwci Bo. So we are waiting on just one more …'

Then came the sound of thundering trotters, and out of the rising mist a giant shape lumbered up the road towards them. Lit by moonlight, Aled could see that it was an enormous, hairy sow, completely black from its crinkled snout, all the way to where it should have had a tail. Then Aled noticed there was someone riding on the creature's back; dressed in an ancient, flowing gown that trailed behind her, a headless woman was waving at them.

Aled was trying to comprehend the peculiar scene but all he could think of was that, for something so huge, the tail-less black sow was surprisingly nimble. As it stopped outside Mamgu's house, the immense pig hopped and danced in the road with excitement. It was hard to tell, but the headless woman appeared to be enjoying herself. She held on with one hand like

a rodeo rider, leaning far back and swinging her arm around above where her head should have been.

Aled stood there staring in awe at the bizarre collection of characters now gathered outside his Mamgu's house: the King in his chariot, a shrivelled old crone, a white lady ghost, the Bwci Bo (a hairy dragon once more), and a headless woman sitting on a giant black pig. Above it all a giant pack of hounds circled in the air yapping impatiently. What was going on?

'Errrk …?' A small voice croaked behind Aled.

Aled turned to see Ethan, dressed in his bin bag, gaping at the scene in disbelief and looking as if he might cry.

'Oh …' said Aled, and he glanced at the amazing display of magic and monsters. 'I'm … um … just out with some friends trick-or-treating.' Aled smiled weakly. 'The costumes are really good aren't they? Anyway. Still no chocolate I'm afraid … but the night is young!'

The Green King moved forward drawn by the dragon horse. 'The Hunt must begin, Aled. Climb aboard.' And the King motioned to a space next to him on the grand chariot.

Anything to get away from the pitiful look on Ethan's face, thought Aled, and he climbed up to stand next to the King. The Bwci Bo took the form of a hideous, bald bird-thing and perched itself in front of him on the chariot.

The Green King put an elaborately decorated horn to his mouth and blew a piercing, earsplitting note and Aled covered his ears. The sound of the horn echoed off the hills, and the Hounds of Annwn barked and howled with excitement.

In what looked like a sudden firework display in the air above the hounds, dozens of elves of all shapes and sizes popped into existence, and dropped onto the backs of the yowling beasts.

'Hang on a minute. Hunt? I don't agree with hunting. What are we hunting?'

'Children!' declared the King, and with that he yanked on the reins of the chariot.

'WHAAAAT?' shouted Aled as they shot straight up into the air.

Holding on with all his strength, Aled could see

that all the Hounds of Annwn, ridden by laughing, shouting elves, were bounding eagerly through the air alongside them. On one side Mallt of the Night, shrieking excitedly, was riding a hound near the front of the pack, closely followed by the White Lady on another of the creatures. On the other side flew the tail-less black sow carrying the headless woman. All around was the racket of yowling hounds.

In front of Aled the Bwci Bo held on with his sharp talons and squawked happily.

'What do you mean we're hunting children?' Aled shouted over the noise of the dogs. The King looked down at him and smiled.

'Faerie magic has little to do with "How?", "Why?" and "What?"' And then, seeing the expression in the King's eyes, Aled recognised him.

'You were The Hill!' Aled exclaimed.

'Yes, I appeared to you as The Hill. I can take many forms,' the King explained, chuckling. 'And I do like to play my little games; a bit of Halloween faerie fun. I also needed to know you were suitable for the Wild Hunt.'

'But I don't want to hunt children!' Aled protested.

The King laughed. 'More precisely it is their dreams that we pursue. The dreams of children are powerful and can shape the world for good or ill, and we keep the Balance. On this night we hunt for the wayward and the naughty children. Sometimes *their* dreams need to be … modified.'

'What do you do?' asked Aled.

'We ride the winds of imagination and grant the gift of …'uncanny dreams'.' The King smiled. 'It is the greatest sport!'

'Uncanny dreams? Do you mean nightmares?' asked Aled desperately clinging on as the Wild Hunt screeched and screamed into the moonlit night. The Green King smiled.

The home of every badly behaved child was visited that night, and every naughty child had terrible dreams filled with dragon horses pulling chariots, headless women riding giant tail-less pigs, and cackling old crones leading terrible hounds ridden by shrieking elves.

The hardest thing to understand for those experiencing this nightmare dreadfulness was the presence of the startled boy. In the middle of it all he seemed to be just along for the ride.

For Aled the night had been a constant blur of faerie chaos, noise and uproar, but now the Wild Hunt was coming to a hovering halt high above a large city. Everything was still and dawn was just starting to brighten the sky in the east. Aled hadn't slept all night, and hadn't eaten for a long time, but he felt wide-awake and full of energy.

'It does make me feel a bit guilty to say it, Your Majesty,' said Aled looking up at the Green King. 'But that was definitely the most fun I've had in all my life!' Aled laughed out loud. 'Woohoo!'

The King laughed back. 'Feel no guilt, Aled. Those many bewildered children will be better people after our night's work … Probably.'

The chariot started to descend, leaving the Wild Hunt above them in a cloud.

The old crone called down from the back of a hound: 'Farewell mortal!' Beside her the headless woman on the tail-less black sow waved, and the sow grunted happily. The elves whooped their farewell.

'Goodbye, child,' said the White Lady as Aled and

the King descended, and the Hunt disappeared from view in the cloudy haze above.

They landed on dewy grass, and in the misty darkness the first dawn birds were starting to sing.

'This is where we part, young Aled,' said the King smiling. 'I have enjoyed our time together, at The Hill, and on the Hunt.'

Aled got down off the chariot. The staggering experiences of the night were just starting to sink in, and he looked up at the Green King wanting to express his gratitude, but something made him look around in the mist. Aled could just make out giant beech trees standing tall and straight, and a sudden panic rose in him.

'Hey!' he exclaimed. 'I don't live here!'

The King laughed a bellowing laugh. 'Do not be the Mighty Worrier! Take care of Now, and the Future take will take care of itself.' And with that, still laughing, he vanished.

'Oh … My … Goodness …' said Aled, looking at the empty space where the King had just been, as it filled with swirling fog. He didn't have a clue where he was or how to get home.

'Yalp!' Aled looked down to see the hairy dragon looking back at him.

'Bwci Bo,' he said, surprised at how happy he felt to see the little monster.

'We're lost, Bo,' said Aled seeing nothing beyond the hazy trees at the edge of the field. 'I don't know where to go from here.'

Bwci Bo looked up at Aled happily, then turned and toddled off into the mist.

'Hey! We've got to stick together,' Aled called. He rushed through the damp grass to catch up with the scampering creature. The dawn light was growing and now he thought he could make out a cottage in the gloom ahead. As he drew closer he noticed that it looked very old, but somehow strangely new at the same time.

Bwci Bo stopped at the door and sat looking at it. Aled knocked.

Soon there was the faint sound of footsteps and the latch lifting, and the door slowly opened.

'At last … Welcome back!' There, standing happily in front of them was the Bwbach from the storeroom. Aled gaped at the small figure standing in the

doorway. Bwci Bo jumped with excitement, zapping between shapes.

'Come in! Come in!' said the Bwbach.

In a daze Aled entered the cottage followed by the Bwci Bo, and he was stunned again. As his eyes adjusted to the gloom he noticed that in the middle of the main room of the cottage was a long, dark wooden table. On the table were clay jugs, wooden bowls, and an unlit candle. Beyond the table was an ancient grandfather clock standing against the wall. This was the place he had visited in the school store room.

The Bwbach closed the door behind them and Aled stood by the crackling fireplace and looked around exasperated.

'Where am I?' asked Aled.

'My cottage is one of the everlasting Houses of Fagan,' explained the Bwbach. 'The Houses hold many stories, and much magic at this time of year, as you have discovered I think.'

There was a knock on the door, and the Bwbach went over to answer it as if expecting more visitors.

'Welcome to my humble cottage, Your Ladyship,'

Aled heard him say to whoever was outside. The Bwbach bowed low and into the cottage glided a tall, hooded figure.

'Hello, Aled,' it said. The figure settled on a chair by the fire and pulled back its hood.

'Miss Ceridwen!' exclaimed Aled.

'Indeed,' she acknowledged with a smile. She bent and scratched the Bwci Bo behind its hairy dragon ear. 'You had an interesting night?' she said looking up at Aled, trying to hide her amusement.

'Yes. I went around delivering nightmares to naughty children,' he said excitedly. 'It was brilliant! The Green King said it was your Halloween gift to me.'

'It was a gift, but not just for you, Aled. You shared it with the other boy.'

'The other boy?' Aled asked confused.

'Yes, the one called Ethan.'

'Ethan? The bully? How did I share it with him?'

'Do you remember what you said when you entered the school yesterday; *"Please new school, please be kind to me. Help me not to be afraid in this new place,"*

she said in Aled's voice. 'It was that appeal, made on Halloween, that called me to your school.

'Ethan said something similar on his first day, but unlike you he decided his best form of defence was attack, and so he is without friends.

'Last night you delivered his gift personally with the help of this clever little Bwci Bo.' She scratched the creature under its chin. 'Ethan also needed to stop believing everything he thought.'

Aled stood in astonishment, recalling the night before.

'Anyway,' said Miss Ceridwen, 'the class is outside on their school trip, and we can't sit around here all day chatting. Are you coming, Aled?' she got up from the chair. 'I shall take my leave of you, Master Bwbach, and your charming cottage. Very well done, and you too clever Bwci Bo. The Green King is very pleased.'

'The class is outside?' asked Aled puzzled. 'But it's only just dawn.'

'It is not dawn any more, Aled. It is lunchtime,' said Miss Ceridwen, and she handed Aled a bar of chocolate. 'Around the everlasting Houses of Fagan the rules of Time can twist and curve. But don't forget, Aled, the most important time is always Now.' She smiled at him, then turned and walked out into the autumn sunshine.

'Thank you very much for your visit, Master Aled,' said the Bwbach. 'It brought Her Ladyship here and that is always a special honour.'

Aled looked down at the little Bwbach.

'No, thank *you* Mr. Bwbach. You woke the Bwci Bo for me and gave me the strangest and best day and night of my life!' Aled looked at the hairy little dragon, and its big damp eyes looked back at him.

The Bwbach looked at the Bwci Bo: 'Do you remember, Master Aled, that I said the Bwci Bo was between homes?'

'Yes, I remember,' said Aled.

'Well … I think I know where it wants its home to be,' said the Bwbach, and Aled understood.

'Really?' Aled said, laughing and excited. 'Bwci Bo, do you want to come home with me?'

'Rrrrrice pudding!' declared the excited Bwci Bo. It leapt up, changing into a small scruffy dog as it flew, and Aled caught it in his arms. The Bwbach opened the cottage door and Aled, struggling to hold the Bwci Bo still as it licked his face, walked out into the bright day.

'Do come and visit again, Master Aled, and you too Bwci Bo,' said the cheery Bwbach standing on the doorstep and waving.

In the distance Aled could see his classmates seated at picnic tables and he made his way over to them. Sitting on a table on his own was Ethan, looking miserable.

'Hiya, Ethan,' said Aled cheerfully. 'Mind if I sit here?'

As Aled sat, Ethan looked at the scruffy dog with sudden horror. 'Oh, don't mind Bo,' reassured Aled. 'It doesn't bite.' Aled looked at the creature uncertainly. 'At least … I don't think it does.

'Anyway, I brought you this,' said Aled, and he handed Ethan the bar of chocolate given to him by Ceridwen in the cottage. 'I did promise.'

Ethan looked at it in amazement.

'You want to give me this when you don't have to?' said Ethan faintly. 'Why?'

'Because Now is very important, and right Now

58

I can make a new friend,' said Aled, smiling. Ethan smiled back as he took the chocolate.

'Thank you,' he said, and broke it in half to share with Aled.

Glossary

Bwci Bo

The Bwci Bo hides in dark places from where it jumps out to scare the unwary. It tends to avoid daylight, preferring to be most active at night. A Bwci Bo is said to be a 'shapeshifter', being able to take whatever form it likes. Usually it turns itself into something horrible just for the fun of it.

Bwbach

A Bwbach is a variety of house elf, which is fiercely protective of its adoptive home. It can be mischievous, though if well treated the Bwbach is a good-natured creature. If sufficiently appreciated by the household, it will happily perform tasks around the home. It is especially fond of fresh cream.

Gwyn ap Nudd

Gwyn ap Nudd is king of the Otherworld, which is also called Annwn. The Tylwyth Teg, the fairy folk, inhabit Annwn and are called the Children of Annwn.

Cŵn Annwn (The Hounds of Annwn)

These are phantom dogs from Annwn, the Otherworld, and are also known as Cŵn Wybr. Gwyn ap Nudd leads them on the Wild Hunt.

Yr Hwch Ddu Gwta (The Tail-less Black Sow)

A terrible spirit called Yr Hwch Ddu Gwta takes the form of a tail-less black sow. She is seen wondering the countryside in the company of a headless woman.

Y Ladi Wen (The White Lady)

Y Ladi Wen is a ghost dressed all in white. She appears to naughty children to warn them of the consequences of their bad behaviour.

Mallt y Nos (Matilda of the Night)

Mallt y Nos is an old crone who is sometimes seen riding with Gwyn ap Nudd and the hounds of the otherworld. She drives the hounds onward with unearthly shrieks and wails.

Dail Eiddew (Ivy Leaves)

A few leaves of ground ivy is said to give you the power to see hags. For dreams of prophecy a child should cut ten ivy leaves, throw away one and put the rest under their pillow before they sleep.

CONTENTS

INTRODUCTION

Are you feeling like you might have bitten off more than you can chew? It's a serious responsibility being best man. There's a lot to do, a lot to remember and, of course, during the speech, a lot to say.

You'll be pleased to know that you don't have to embark on your new duties completely alone. The in-depth advice you'll find in this book will make your task much easier. Follow my step-by-step advice and, with a bit of luck, everything will go swimmingly. The book is divided into two parts – Part One deals with everything except the speech, from the appointment to the wedding day, and Part Two focuses on the speech itself.

The following areas are covered in detail:

PART ONE

- The appointment of the best man: let the groom know he's chosen the right man.
- Dealing diplomatically with the in-laws: this sometimes calls for supreme tact.
- The engagement party: your first chance to meet everyone involved in the wedding.
- Organising and executing a brilliant stag party: how to do it with military precision and ensure everyone has a great time.
- A step-by-step guide to the best man's duties in the run-up to the wedding: there's a lot more to remember than just the ring.
- The wedding rehearsal: your last chance to smooth out any potential problems.
- The actual ceremony: how to look after the groom, organise the ushers and direct the guests.
- The reception: there could be anything from 20–200 guests, and you're expected to help look after them.
- The end of the party: oversee the departure of the guests and help the happy couple get away on their honeymoon.

✦ PART TWO

- The speech: how to write, practise and deliver a funny and unforgettable speech.

The advice given in this book will help you no matter what type of wedding you are taking part in as many of the best man's duties are the same whatever the scale/venue/religion etc. Just pick out the parts that are relevant to the type of wedding that you are going to be involved in. In Chapter 7 (see pages 70–75) I have detailed some of the wedding customs of different cultures, religions etc.

✧ ORIGINS OF THE ROLE

There are several theories as to how the role of best man first came about. Some believe the role traces its origins back to the time of the Germanic Goths during the latter days of the Roman Empire. Back then it was usual for a man to marry within his own community. But often there weren't enough women to go round in which case nuptially-inclined young men were forced to look elsewhere for a bride. This called for visits to women in neighbouring villages. Hardly surprisingly, these unsuspecting women (not to mention their irate fathers) didn't look too kindly upon being kidnapped by a hairy Goth. Along with their families they often put up quite a fight. It was the best man's job to physically support the potential groom during the kidnap process, and later at the ceremony when the bride's father and brothers would often turn up to wrestle the girl back.

Nowadays we'd hope that most brides, and most fathers of the bride for that matter, would have given their consent to the marriage. Therefore the best man's support is more moral and emotional than physical. But during the ceremony he still stands on the right of his groom and the bride, ready to defend them, should the need arise.

This book won't instruct you how to fight off the bride's irate family (I'll leave you to figure that one out for yourself should the unfortunate situation arise), but what it will do is help you to be the best best man you can possibly be.

PART ONE

BEST MAN'S DUTIES

CHAPTER 1

THE APPOINTMENT

It rarely comes completely out of the blue.
Unless you're old friends who haven't seen one
another in years, or you live across the other
side of the world, it's likely you will see the
occasion of your appointment coming. It
normally happens like this: a couple of weeks
after your friend has announced that he and
his girlfriend are getting engaged you get a
low-key invitation to meet him at the pub.
"Nothing special," he says, "just you and me
for a quiet drink." The instant you realise that
the rest of the lads won't be coming too, you
should smell a rat. This isn't going to be any
ordinary drink. You need to go along prepared
for this one. It's going to be the big question.

The appointment of the best man can be a scary task – both for the intended best man and for the future groom. I've heard of grooms getting themselves in a terrible state over the whole situation. How should I go about doing it? What if my best man doesn't want to be my best man? What if he doesn't approve of my wife? Some fiancés approach the best man proposal with almost as much dread as the actual marriage proposal. This is just silly. There's no need to make a song and a dance out of it. It's highly likely that you, the future best man, know you're going to be asked. And it's also highly likely that the future groom knows that you know you're going to be asked. Just make sure you make things as comfortable as you can for your groom when he asks you and put him at ease. It's not like he has to get down on one knee with a ring and a bunch of roses! Just buying you a few drinks should suffice.

Oh, and don't hesitate too long before you accept the job. In all but the very rarest of situations you should have seen the request coming and you should already have made up your mind. If you ask for a few days to ponder it over then the groom will never be entirely sure that you are truly committed to your role. One short-lived best man I once knew took over a week to get back to his friend after he was originally asked. By the time he gave his answer, which incidentally was 'Yes', the groom had already appointed someone else. They were never quite the same close friends ever again.

✧ BE COMMITTED

So let's presume you have accepted your role. Let's face it, if you'd turned him down you'd hardly be reading this book, would you? The first thing you should do is convince the groom that you are 100 per cent committed to being the best best man possible. Tell him what a great woman he is marrying and remind him that you are available to help both of them with the wedding preparations in any way you can.

You should arrange to meet with the couple as soon as possible to get an idea of the kind of wedding it is going to be and to discuss exactly what duties they want you to undertake. This is a good chance to show the bride-to-be what a superb organiser you are, how responsible you can be, how cool you are under pressure and how willing you are to help. Getting married is an extremely stressful period in any couple's life. Don't forget that you are there to help things go smoothly – both on the wedding day and in the months leading up to it.

I know of one best man who was faced with a very tricky situation indeed. His soon-to-be-married friends were finding that their wedding plans were spiralling completely out of control and causing a lot of unnecessary tension between them. At this stressful time, even the smallest things can cause a disagreement. The best man found himself having to step in at various hairy moments to calm things down when the couple started arguing about caterers, florists, parents-in-law, page boys, table plans, the colour of the napkins etc, etc. Without taking sides, 'bestie' managed to settle virtually every dispute they had. (The napkin colour dilemma, however, was never properly resolved and, to this day, the groom still cannot tell the difference between burnt orange and fuchsia.) Other friends now reckon best man may have saved their marriage before it had even started. Fortunately bride and groom are still happily married. They are forever grateful to him for his delicate mediation skills.

✧ MEET THE PARENTS

As the best man you should make contact with both the bride's and groom's parents early on in the engagement. You'll meet the parents at the engagement party of course, but it's a good idea to visit them, or at least speak to them on the phone, beforehand. The more people that are reassured of how competent and responsible you are, the smoother the whole wedding build-up and day will be. Even if you already know one or both sets of parents, talk to the bride and groom before making contact. You should tread carefully if the parents are separated or there are step-parents involved; again check with the bride and groom as to who you should be making contact with.

✧ QUALITIES A BEST MAN NEEDS
Marriage status

Tradition used to demand that the best man should be a bachelor. That way, if the groom was (due to various unforseen circumstances, like a change of mind or death) unable to fulfil his duty and marry his bride, then the best man could step in and fill his shoes. Nowadays, you'll be happy to know, you are no longer required to act as replacement groom and no one will expect you to be unmarried. In fact, if you've already been through the marriage experience yourself, you're likely to make a better go of it as best man. You'll know exactly what the groom's up against.

Sobriety

No one wants to hear a slurred best man's speech. It may be funny for the first couple of minutes, but after a while the guests will lose their patience.

You've also got to maintain a certain level-headedness during the stag celebrations. Of course you're not expected to remain completely sober, but it is up to you to get the groom back home in one piece. This means you'll have to be sober enough to at least dial the number of a taxi firm on your mobile phone.

Punctuality

Some grooms are so nervous that they lose the ability to tell the time, let alone remember to put on their watch the morning of the big day. Timekeeping is very much your job. If the groom is late you'll get the blame. If the ushers are late you'll get the blame. If you're late, no one will speak to you for the rest of the day.

Responsibility

There's no doubting that it's stressful being a best man. With so many things to remember and organise, there are going to be times when you wonder why you agreed to take on the job. But with lots of preparation and clear-thinking you'll make the groom and his wife a very happy couple and you'll have a great day yourself. If you're methodical you can make sure there are no mishaps.

Tact

After the bride and groom, you are the person next in line in the spotlight. Like it or not, people will be watching you. You will already know a lot of the guests, and no one's expecting you to put on airs, but there are certain times when you will need to be very tactful. For example, it's your job to get everyone from the marriage venue to the reception. When you deliver your speech you need to remember that your audience ranges from five-year-old bridesmaids to 95-year-old grannies. A certain diplomacy will be expected. Don't be prudish, but do be prudent.

Presentability

A friend of mine insisted on choosing his best friend as his best man. Nothing unusual about that you might think. Except when I tell you that his best friend was scruffy, drunken and unhygienic. We all warned the groom, but he wouldn't have any of it. He dug his heels in and appointed his unkempt friend as best man. It was a case of the groom and the ungroomed.

Sure enough, the big day came and there was the best man with a shabby suit, old, unpolished shoes, loosened tie, scraggly, greasy hair, and a cigarette permanently lodged in the side of his mouth. Fortunately the tails of his morning suit hid the fact that his shirt wasn't even tucked in.

If your usual style could be described as scruffy, shabby or scraggly – or indeed any other word that means the same thing – you're going to have to accept that you'll have to undergo a bit of a makeover.

Communication skills

Communicating with people is one of your key jobs on the day – sorting out the ushers, making sure that the guests are OK, directing people to the reception venue and, of course, the speech. Although other people will make speeches at the wedding, it is the best man's speech that is the most anticipated. This doesn't, however, mean that you have to be a stand-up comedian or a latter-day Martin Luther King. No one is expecting a professional level address. They want to laugh, yes. They perhaps want to be moved somewhat. But they all know you are a normal bloke who happens to be very good friends with the groom.

If you feel your communication skills could use a little work, then you can always practise them to build up your confidence. More on that later (see page 77).

CHAPTER 2

ENGAGEMENT PARTY

Not every couple will have an engagement party. If they don't then in some ways you can count yourself lucky – that's one less best man duty on your list of things to do. But if they do then it's crucial that you attend. After the bride, groom and their immediate family members, you and the maid of honour are the next most important guests. Turn up and turn up on time.

View the engagement party as your first chance to gauge just how things might pan out on the big day. It's by no means a rehearsal (most engagement parties are simply a chance for all the friends and family to meet and share a few drinks) but it will give you an invaluable insight into potential pitfalls and problem family members. It will also give you the chance to meet many of the other wedding guests.

18

This is the evening when you first meet the bride's antisocial brother. This is your chance to witness Auntie Dot's gin-drinking abilities first hand. This is also when you can really shine and reassure both sets of parents that you are without doubt the best man for the job. Make an effort to circulate and find out who's who. It will make things easier on the wedding day when you have to inform Sally and Mark that their three-year-old son is systematically dismantling the wedding cake.

I heard of a very posh engagement party a couple of years ago when the bride's and groom's parents met for the first time. It was on neutral territory and everyone expected proceedings to run as smoothly as the copious supply of alcohol. That was the problem. There was too much alcohol. The bride's mother had about three bottles of champagne to herself and made what she thought was a fairly innocuous comment about the groom's mother's party dress. The latter took offence and uttered similar comments about the former's hair-do. Needless to say, maternal relations remained frosty until well after the wedding day.

But because the best man was aware of this initial personality clash it meant that he was able to keep both mothers apart on the wedding day and thereby avoid unnecessary confrontation. If the best man belongs to neither family he is in the prime position to act as go-between and peace negotiator; a delicate task indeed.

Incidentally, the way you present yourself during the engagement party is crucial. If you turn up late in scruffy clothes and proceed to drink the bar dry then everyone concerned will spend the run-up to the wedding worrying that you'll do the same on the big day. Reassure the bride, groom and both families by playing it cool.

CHAPTER 3

STAG PARTY

What used to be a single evening spent in a pub followed by some very inept dancing in a nightclub, has now turned into a major social event, often lasting over a long weekend. There may be three evenings to coordinate, two activity days to arrange, flights abroad that need to be booked and 20 rowdy stags who need marshalling. Some stags even have two stag dos – perhaps a small evening party for work colleagues and then a weekend for close friends. Whatever your plans turn out to be, believe me, the whole event needs to be organised with military precision, otherwise it will soon descend into chaos.

The stag do is what separates best men from worst men. It is where you will stand or fall. Aside from the wedding speech, it is the duty that you will be most remembered for and most judged on. Make sure you get it right and plan early.

CHOOSING THE STAGS

One thing you can guarantee about all of the groom's closest friends is that they will not necessarily get on with each other as well as they get on with the groom. How on earth can you expect Ian the IT expert to have anything in common with Mad Dog Mitchell? When coming up with a list of stags, there's no point simply asking the groom for a list of his top 15 friends. There are some far more tricky aspects to consider.

1   Will they make an effort to get on with the other stags?
    The last thing you want on the stag do is for the group to split into several small cliques. I have a friend who was brought up in France

and who finished his schooling in Britain. Rather foolishly he invited both his French and British friends on his stag do. Through no fault of their own, other than an inability to comprehend one another, the group immediately split into two and the groom was left trying to bridge the gap. He spent more of the weekend translating jokes that were barely funny in the first place than he did enjoying himself. It would have been far better if he'd thrown two stag parties – one for the Frogs and one for the Ros-Bifs.

2   Can they afford it?
    With stag weekends regularly costing up to £1,000 per person nowadays, especially if foreign flights are involved, there's nothing more embarrassing than arriving at your destination only to find that a couple of guys have already run out of money. On my own stag weekend, one of my best friends was unemployed at the time and couldn't afford to stay in our hotel with us. He ended up sleeping in the back of his car which inevitably broke up the group somewhat. He also looked and smelled like he'd slept in a ditch. In fact, come to think of it, maybe he did sleep in a ditch?

3   Does the groom know this guy well enough to go out on his own for a drink with him?
    There's no point inviting transient friends along. A stag do is a chance for the groom to officially acknowledge someone as a close friend. A bloke he hit it off with down the pub last week does not count.

4   Will he add to the groom's enjoyment of the stag do?
    Your groom really won't want to spend time wishing he hadn't invited a certain person along. This is well worth remembering if he plans to invite old friends he hasn't seen or been in contact with for ages. I heard about one groom who asked along an old friend from primary school who had since emigrated to Australia. It seems the friend had spent the intervening years decorating himself with rather unsavoury tattoos and cultivating a serious drinking habit. Fortunately for the rest of the stags he

spent most of the weekend curled up in a drunken heap on the floor of his hotel room.

In times past it was traditional to invite both the groom's and the bride's father along on the stag do. No one will expect you to do that nowadays. Okay, so it might work if you're marrying Ozzy Osbourne's daughter – in fact it would even liven up proceedings – but most of the stags would think it odd if there was a paternal element to the party. Especially if that paternal element was the one giving away the bride. Whatever they said, other stags would feel distinctly uncomfortable sharing a rowdy evening with the groom's father or future father-in-law. What if a visit to a strip club was part of the evening's entertainment?

Having said this, it is of course a matter of personal choice for the groom. He and his friends may get on so well with his father that it would be odd not to invite him along. Indeed his Dad might be an Ozzy Osbourne wannabe, but do think about what effect his presence will have on the party.

It's a good idea to invite along any brother of the bride. The groom may not yet be friends with his future brother-in-law, in which case the latter will probably make his excuses. But it would certainly be very politic to give him the choice.

Choosing the right stags is a complicated business. It's well worth setting aside a whole evening to sit down with the groom and finalise the invitation list. Think of the stag do as a cooking recipe. If you don't get the correct ingredients (i.e. the right stags) then you haven't got a chance of creating a tasty dish that everyone will enjoy.

✧ DECIDING WHAT DO DO

It doesn't even have to be a boozy, raucous affair if this isn't the groom's style and there's nothing wrong with simply making an evening of it in your local town, having a meal and a few drinks. But most grooms want something a bit more adventurous nowadays. If everyone can afford it, why not spend a long weekend somewhere? Why not go abroad for a couple of days to Barcelona, Prague, Amsterdam or Dublin? Or if you're feeling really flush, maybe New York or Las Vegas?

The revolution in air travel, particularly short-haul, means it's now so much cheaper and easier to fly to a foreign destination. Travel companies have realised how much potential there is in both the stag and the hen weekend market. If you let a professional stag organisation company help you out it may cost a bit more, but you'll cut down on your list of best man duties.

Spending a weekend away is a great leveller and the perfect way to get all the stags bonding. If no one has been to the destination before and, even better, if you're abroad and no one speaks the local lingo, then you'll find that everyone rallies together in the face of a common enemy, so to speak. People are also far more likely to let their hair down and act like fools when they're in a foreign country – which is a successful ingredient to any stag weekend.

I have a friend who is a lawyer and one of the most cautious, law-abiding men I know. Partly because of his profession he never steps out of line and wouldn't dream of misbehaving in public. Yet the two times I've been abroad on stag weekends with him I've finally seen his true colours emerge.

25

Away from home he knew his job was not at risk if he was to over-indulge on the booze and have a minor brush with the law. In fact, despite a severe lack of sobriety, he actually managed to remain in control. But just the knowledge that he could really let loose if he wanted to meant he had a far more enjoyable time than normal. And, of course, in turn, so did everyone else.

Ultimately it's the groom's decision as to where you all go and what you do. He will, however, appreciate guidance from you. Don't pressurise him into doing anything or going anywhere he'd prefer not to. Although you're organising the do, this is his celebration and your main concern is that he has a great time. Bear in mind what kind of person he is and what type of stags he is inviting along. Sky-diving, strip clubs and rivers of booze are not everyone's cup of tea. On the following few pages you'll find a few suggestions for stag do fun.

Activity days

Rally driving, paintballing, parachuting, hunting, flying lesson, abseiling, bungee jumping, kayaking, surfing, deep-sea fishing, gliding, go-karting, greyhound racing, horse racing, paragliding, hang gliding, quad bikes, tank driving, water skiing, power boating – and that's just for starters. There are so many activities on offer that are suitable for a stag activity day. If you've got money to burn you can even drive a Formula One car around a racetrack or co-pilot a Russian MIG in the skies above Moscow.

Find out from the groom what kind of activities he'd like to do. And use your email circulars (see page 32) to ascertain how much the other stags are willing to pay. It may end up that you all just go for a round of golf. But the advantage of more extreme activities is that they very quickly break the ice if the stags don't all know one another and, more importantly, they offer tempting chances to play practical jokes and ridicule the groom. Just make sure he doesn't break any bones.

I will never forget the story of the army officer whose best man arranged for him and his army friends to spend a stag weekend in Snowdonia. As you can expect with a group of off-duty soldiers, the mood was fairly boisterous. In his infinite wisdom, 'bestie' had arranged for all the boys to go quad biking over some pretty dangerous Welsh terrain. Stupidly, someone thought it would be a good idea to bring along a crate of beers, most of it destined for the throat of the groom.

You can guess what happened. The groom got drunk, lost control of his quad bike and ended up breaking his left arm. His fellow stags thought it was hilarious, but when the best man had to explain to the bride-to-be what had happened, she almost broke his left arm too.

On activity days it's essential to stay off the booze until the dangerous part is over. If it's just golf you're doing then you can all drink as much as you like (well, within reason unless you want to get thrown off the course). But if the day's action involves motorised vehicles and a certain manual dexterity and a risk of bodily damage, then you're going to need to remain in charge of your faculties. Booze and tank driving or flying lessons simply do not mix. Most stag activity organisers are well trained in spotting, and smelling, anyone who's been drinking.

There are loads of companies out there who will organise a stag activity for you (see pages 120–122). A quick search on the internet will dig up dozens of businesses vying for your custom. Simply type your chosen activity and the word 'stag' into a search engine and see what comes up. Give the company a call and find out a little more about what they do before booking anything. Make sure that the company/operator you use is fully insured against accident and injury.

It sounds obvious, but the best activities for group bonding are the ones where you remain in a group. Driving Formula One cars all day may sound like a great laugh, but it's a solitary activity. Whereas spending all day paintballing may be a bit unadventurous, but at least you're all in a team together. Ultimately it's the company that's more important than the adrenalin.

Sporting events

Getting a large number of tickets for a Premiership football match is about as easy as figuring out why England haven't won the World Cup since 1966. Nevertheless if you book through an agency or you opt for a less popular sport instead you may have more luck. A Saturday afternoon sporting event can be a great way to get the party going, especially if you all have some money riding on the outcome. What about a day at the races?

Golf

Golf is now the number one participation sport on stag dos, partly because it's so sociable and partly because it's easy to handicap everyone and even things out. The only problem is that you'll have to split up a large group of stags – it's impractical to send out groups of more than four players.

As a rule, it's best not to tell the golf club that you are all on a stag do. They'll only worry about drinking on the course and rowdy behaviour. Just tell them it's a business trip and keep your voices down until you're all past the third hole.

You may well have a few non-golfers among your group, but because golf is such an adaptable sport this shouldn't pose too many problems. Here are a few ways to ensure that whatever the skill levels, everyone should get a good hit.

BEST BALL Split the stags into teams. The idea is to make sure each team finishes the round with the lowest score. After each team member has done his first drive the team keeps the best drive and picks up the other balls. The team then all play their second balls from the spot where the best first drive landed. Again they keep the best shot and pick up the other balls before playing them from the position of the best second shot. This continues all the way to the green and until the first player reaches the hole.

THREE CLUB Each player chooses three clubs and three clubs only to use throughout the whole round. You then have to hit your shots using your clubs in strict sequence – no matter what shot you are going for. Laugh at each other as you inevitably end up driving with a putter on certain holes or putting with a driver.

This is a great way to equalise different skill levels and is quite a laugh too, as you can imagine. Some people insist that everyone have the same three clubs: a driver, a sand wedge and a putter. Just don't let the groundsmen spot you.

SPEED GOLF Each player carries just one club with him and has to run around the course in between shots. Don't worry, no one is allowed to play the ball as if it's a hockey match, since points are awarded for both speed and the number of shots required to complete the course. So even though you run, you do have to stop and play each shot properly.

Evening entertainment

This can be more difficult to organise than the daytime activity. If you're intending to have a boozy evening, the presence of vast amounts of alcohol means individual egos soon start to take over. What you don't want is different stags arguing over what the course of action should be. Decide on a plan well beforehand and stick to it. Otherwise the group will split up and the evening will rapidly deteriorate. Remember, you're in charge.

If you're all on a stag weekend then meet up in the hotel bar. Start off with a top-notch meal. Again, if it's going to be a raucous evening rather than a sedate meal with a small glass of port and a cigar, think about asking the hotel/restuarant whether they have a private dining room. These are designed with stag parties in mind since you can get away with the type of boozing and behaviour that wouldn't be tolerated in the main restaurant. Anyone who's seen a group of stags in a restaurant will know full well that no one wants to witness their shenanigans. Nor will many of the stags want their shenanigans witnessed by normal law-abiding people. The table manners alone will be enough to put off other more civilised eaters.

After dinner what you don't want to do is just head off to a drinking establishment. Ideally you need some sort of focus to the evening. Something like a pool tournament or ten pin bowling may not be tremendously exciting, but what about a night of greyhound racing, a rock concert or a trip to the local casino? Oh, and don't make the mistake that a close friend of mine did. As best man he was of course in charge of the kitty (see page 33). The minute he was let loose in the casino he stuck all the money on the roulette table. Of course he lost the lot. He also lost the respect of the groom and all his fellow stags.

Many nightclubs and casinos are distinctly stag-unfriendly. Hardly surprising – the last thing they want is a 15-strong rabble of boozy lads invading their premises. There are two ways to get round this problem. Either call a few days in advance to put your names on the door, or else split the group up into threes and fours and stagger your entry. On my stag weekend my best man had to phone the nightclubs a couple of weeks beforehand and supply the names, addresses and occupations of every member of our party. We still managed to get thrown out of one of them.

Many stag nights end up with some sort of under-dressed female entertainment. It's not every groom's idea of fun – and for goodness sake don't let his bride-to-be find out – but it's the one time in his life when he can look at other naked ladies without feeling guilty or sleazy. It's a centuries-old tradition dating back to ancient Greek times, so it would be churlish not to see some female flesh. But it is of course a

WHAT IF THE BEST MAN IS A WOMAN?

Hey, it's the 21st century. This happens more often nowadays than you'd think. And if a groom's best friend is female, or his sister, as is often the case, why shouldn't he choose her as his best (wo)man?

If you are the best woman, there are certain practicalities to consider: your idea of a stag do is likely to be a little different. It's also unlikely that you'll be keen on visiting a strip club etc. But don't be bothered about this. If the groom expected to be entertained by naked ladies then he wouldn't have asked you to be his best woman. Just think about the plus points of your stag do – it's highly likely that it will be better organised, as women are almost always better than men at organising social events. The other big plus is that as you're new to all this you may well come up with something a lot more original.

A couple of years ago a female friend of my mother's was appointed best woman to her best friend. Her job involved the, at first, rather unenviable task of marshalling 12 rowdy men through the stag evening. Many of them were sceptical that she, as a woman, was up to the job. But instead of opting for the obvious bar, restaurant, bar, nightclub combination, she instead booked everyone into a luxurious spa hotel for the afternoon. For most of the men present it was their first experience of being massaged, pampered, manicured, pedicured and generally beautified. After they had overcome their initial macho cynicism they all began to unwind, had a wonderful time and left relaxed and rejuvenated. Out of respect for tradition, female bestie then took them all down the pub afterwards.

personal choice for the groom. Don't pressurise him. If he wants to abstain, for the sake of his conscience and his wife-to-be, then let him and respect him for it.

✧ ORGANISING THE STAG CELEBRATIONS

Once you've helped the groom to choose his trusty wing men and decided where you're going to go and what you're going to do, it's now up to you to start organising things. Believe me, you can't start early enough on this task.

Traditionally, stag celebrations used to be held on the Thursday or Friday before a Saturday wedding. Don't even think about doing it this close to the wedding. You need as much time as possible for the bruises to heal, the hangover to wear off and the eyebrow hair to grow back. Instead hold it a couple of weekends before the big day. In any case, the evening before the wedding will probably be taken up with a family dinner (see page 50).

Start off by phoning all the chosen stags and extending an official invitation. Make a note of each one's email address and send all of them, including the groom, two or three provisional dates for the big celebration. You can guarantee that not everyone will be able to make the same evening or weekend, but if you offer a few dates then you'll probably be able to accommodate most of the people on the list. There are always a couple of the groom's friends who can't make it. This is unavoidable. You'll just have to decide with the groom whether, as guests, they are so important that you need to reschedule the whole thing. Sometimes on a weekend stag celebration you'll find that certain stags can make part of the weekend but not all of it. This is not ideal, but it's better than not having them come at all. It just means that it's more organising for you.

Keeping track of everyone who has been invited is very complicated. Make a list of who's committed to coming and whether they have covered any payment or deposits that you may need from them. On a stag weekend there will be lots of hotels, restaurants and events to book. Be meticulous and keep a written record of who has paid for what. (See The Financial Side, pages 33–34.)

Set up two circular email lists to all the stags – one which includes the groom and one which doesn't. This way you can keep the groom abreast of all the timings and travel arrangements, but keep him in the dark when it comes to what activities and entertainment are involved and how you plan to really stitch him up. Yes, well and truly stitch him up you must (see Stag Night Practical Jokes pages 36–37). This is all part and parcel of the stag celebrations. No proper stag do is complete without it.

✧ KEEP COMMUNICATING WITH THE STAGS

Send regular emails updating the stags on what's planned, when it's happening and where you'll all be going. Email banter can be a great way for stags initially to get to know one another. It will also get everyone in the mood for the stag celebrations.

Get hold of mobile phone numbers for everyone coming on the stag do. Plug all these numbers into your own phone. On a stag weekend, especially if you're moving around, it's easy to lose the odd person. You need to keep the troops together at all times.

You're not required to be everyone's babysitter, but if foreign travel is involved then check that everyone has set up their phones to function abroad. It may also be an idea to remind them all to check they have travel insurance.

✧ THE FINANCIAL SIDE

Get a firm commitment from everyone invited as soon as possible. You may be required to put down a deposit on hotel accommodation and pay for flights well in advance. Unless you have a particularly generous bank manager, you'll need to get cheques from everyone to cover this. The financial side of the stag do can be the most stressful part. I would advise you not to book anything until you have received money from all, or virtually all of the stags. It is always the best man who ends up paying for any shortfall. And you can't exactly ask the groom to pay for financially errant friends.

In fact, with the possible exception of foreign flights, the groom traditionally shouldn't pay for anything. No one will mind if you spread out all of his costs among you and the rest of the stags. Between 10 or 15 of you this won't work out to be a huge amount. The groom will probably be spending huge amounts of his own money on his wedding and will appreciate the gesture.

One area that can be tricky to organise is the buying of drinks. Let's face it: on most stag dos there is going to be drinking. If the rounds of drinks aren't seen to be fair, some of the stags are going to get upset. The way to deal with this is to use the whip-round system. At the beginning of the evening or weekend ask all the stags (except for the groom, of course) to hand over enough money for say 10 drinks. Collect that money together, add your own contribution and place it all in one wallet that you'll then keep in a safe pocket. From then on the wallet will be known as 'the kitty' and all drinks should be bought using money from it.

CAMERAS OR NO CAMERAS?

The groom does not want to worry about pictures of him appearing on a website the day before he gets married. He certainly doesn't want his bride or her family to see evidence of his stag do exploits.

You can't, of course, ban cameras from the stag weekend. In fact you'll want to record some of the funnier incidents during the daytime activities. But, as best man, you should ensure that no photographic devices are anywhere to be seen once the sun's gone down. In any case, blow-up dolls and inflatable sheep never look their best under flash exposure.

Since there may be 10 or 15 stags, inevitably different people will drink at different speeds. While Mad Dog Mitchell, for example, can down three pints in 20 minutes, Ian the IT expert may well take a whole hour to get through a small glass of white wine. This, I am afraid, is all part and parcel of a lively stag do. It's tough luck, really, for the slow drinkers. What you cannot be expected to do, as best man, is to monitor who's drinking what and who owes how much to the kitty. Everyone has to simply enter into the spirit of things and donate the same amount, regardless of how much they plan to consume. If you think this may cause problems then you should warn people before the start of the stag do.

I remember being at one stag evening in a very expensive drinking club. The majority of the stags rather wisely stuck to beer for most of the evening, but a couple of jokers thought they'd spend all night downing champagne, expensive cocktails and fine brandies. It was funny at first, but since we were all in a whip-round, some people soon got a little annoyed. What you don't want is resentment on a stag do because someone isn't pulling his weight financially. In fact, what normally happens is that the kitty soon runs out and those that are drinking less go to bed before the hard core contingent. Late drinkers then do a second whip-round and start up another kitty. But of course you don't want the group splitting off early into different cliques and buying rounds separately. The whole idea of a stag do is for the groom's best friends to bond together before he gets married. This means drinking together, too.

✦ MEETING UP

If the stag do is just an evening out then this is easy. Meet in a centrally located pub and start the night from there. But where should you meet up if you're all embarking on a stag weekend?

One great way to get the party going is to hire a limousine to transport you all to the stag venue (see page 122). Meet in a pub and arrange for the limo driver to pick you all up after work on a Friday. Then bundle everyone into the limo, champagne and all. By the time you reach your destination you'll all have a few drinks inside you and everyone in the group will know one another. Once you've split the cost of the limo between all of you it might actually work out cheaper than taking the train.

For domestic stag weekends the train is of course the other option. Nearly every large railway station has a pub or bar. They're hardly the most refined of establishments (at the beginning of my stag weekend we had trouble persuading the station tramp that he wasn't invited along too), but you'll find they are the perfect meeting points.

There is no chance on earth that all the stags will arrive on time. As they turn up at staggered intervals from different parts of town, as best man you'll be glad that you have a base where everyone can meet. This is the opportunity for any stags who don't already know one another to break the ice.

For stag weekends abroad, the airport pubs and bars are the best places to meet. It's worth considering paying that little bit extra and booking everyone into the business or first class lounge. You don't have to be flying luxury to avail yourselves of these places. Just phone ahead and book the group in. But a word of caution. Don't tell them you're all on a stag trip. Say it's a business golfing trip instead. And take it easy on the sauce. Airline operators won't let you on the plane nowadays if they suspect you're drunk. It's just not worth the security risk.

✦ DON'T OVERDO THE BOOZE

No one is expecting you to stay sober – that would be patently ridiculous. Besides, you'll be expected to get things going on the

STAG NIGHT PRACTICAL JOKES

First of all it's traditional to make the groom wear utterly embarrassing clothing for the crucial stages of the stag do. A simple way to do this is to buy some tasteless clothing in a charity shop the day before the stag weekend starts. Force the groom to wear these clothes during the daytime and/or the evening entertainment. (See page 123 for party supplies.)

Comedy breasts are always a big favourite, as is an old floral pattern dress and women's underwear. The character and spirit of your groom will determine just how outrageous a costume you can make him wear. It takes a real man to wear drag on his stag do and his friends will respect him forever if he does.

On my own stag weekend I was forced to wear a tight, sleeveless belly-button T-shirt with the word 'Princess' emblazoned across the front, a pair of pink baggy trousers and a little purple clip-on bow tie. Then, to my embarrassment, I learned we were to spend the evening at a greyhound track. The shaven-haired, tattooed men at the racetrack bar raised a few eyebrows, but fortunately I got through the evening unscathed.

If the groom does agree to wear women's clothing and carry an inflatable sheep round all night (under peer pressure it's not like he'll have a choice) he will feel a lot better if everyone else makes a bit of an effort too. Why not get T-shirts printed up for all the rest of the stags to wear? (See page 123 for companies that offer this service.) This way the groom will look more like the butt of a practical joke and less like a deranged person who got dressed in the dark.

But don't forget that if an upmarket bar or nightclub is part of the evening's entertainment, then you will all need smart clothes to change into later. However much

drinks front and encourage a party atmosphere from the very start. However, you don't want to get blind drunk. If anyone's, that's the job of the groom. Remember that you're in charge of the evening, from start to finish. You've got to get everyone together at the beginning and you've got to get the groom home at the end of the evening. He may have drunk so much that he can barely remember his own name, let alone where he's staying that night. It's your job to get him tucked up safely in bed in one piece.

Oh, and if your stag evening is taking place in the same town that his fiancée lives in, whatever you do, don't let him get ideas about going home to her after a boozy evening. Can you imagine her face when he turns up at her door at 3am, dishevelled and stinking of booze. In fact, don't even let him call her. His you charm the bouncer, he will not let a man wearing a dress and comedy breasts pass through his doors.

Any groom worth his salt will expect some sort of practical joke. Strippers dressed as policewomen; shaved eyebrows; groom handcuffed half-naked to a lamppost; groom abandoned with no phone and no money... the list of ideas is long and there are always laughs to be had at the groom's expense. Just don't take the joke too far – as the best man you know the groom well and should judge what he will and won't find amusing. Also consider what the bride's reaction will be. The basic rules are: don't do anything that is going to affect his appearance for the wedding or anything potentially terrifying/injurious/dangerous. Practical jokes are supposed to add to the enjoyment of the evening, not frighten the groom to death and spoil the wedding photos.

I heard of one stag weekend recently in Estonia, in eastern Europe. The stag party had just arrived at the activity centre where they'd booked a day of military games when suddenly a van screeched to a halt in front of them. Out of the back of the van jumped five huge thugs armed with rifles and wearing balaclavas. They promptly grabbed the groom, man-handled him into the back of the van and drove off into the woods.

It turned out that the best man had arranged the kidnapping as part of an elaborate practical trick. The poor groom had no idea and assumed he was about to come to an awful end, miles from home, courtesy of a bullet from a Mafia boss's Kalashnikov. Unfortunately for all concerned he decided his only course of action was to fight his way out of the back of the van. He managed to inflict some serious punches on the actors he believed were Mafia thugs, but when he heroically jumped from the moving van he broke his collar bone.

He laughed about it all afterwards... several months afterwards.

slurred speech will only make her worry he's done something he shouldn't have.

An old friend of mine had his stag night in London and never even considered that it might be a good idea to stay somewhere other than at his (and his fiancée's) flat. Before the wedding I witnessed her berating the best man for letting his protegé get in the state he did. Apparently she had been woken up at 4am by her husband-to-be banging on their front door. When she opened it he staggered in dressed in nothing but his underpants and a ripped, lipstick-stained shirt. His breath smelt like a distillery. In order to avoid incurring the wrath of the fiancée, the best man had deposited the drunken groom outside his flat and driven off in a taxi. Needless to say, the fiancée's wrath had lasted for a good few days.

CHAPTER 4

COUNTDOWN TO
THE BIG DAY

The countdown to the wedding is a bit like a NASA countdown to the launch of one of their rockets. The schedule takes eons of planning and starts to get more and more demanding the nearer you get to take-off. The weeks before the wedding are always fraught with stress for both the bride and the groom. No wedding would be complete without these last minute hiccups.

Your job is to help iron out as many of the problems as possible, be on hand whenever you can to help and act as a sympathetic ear when it all simply gets too much.

Here's a general idea of what you can expect in your role
as best man in the run-up to the wedding.

12 MONTHS TO GO

✧ You are appointed as best man.
✧ Make a note in your diary of wedding date
  and keep week before wedding clear as
  your services will be needed!

9 MONTHS TO GO

✧ Engagement party.

5 MONTHS TO GO

✧ Help groom to choose the ushers.
✧ Start organising the stag party/weekend.

4 MONTHS TO GO

✧ Discuss wedding plans with the bride and
  groom so that you know who other
  members of wedding party are etc.
✧ Make sure you know what the transport
  arrangements are.
✧ Go with groom to choose wedding outfits.

3 MONTHS TO GO

✧ Start writing your speech.
✧ Buy gift and card for the wedding couple.

2 MONTHS TO GO

✧ Regularly practise your speech.
✧ Confirm all of the arrangements for the stag
  party/weekend.

4 WEEKS TO GO

✧ The stag party/weekend.

3 WEEKS TO GO

✧ Prepare and send duty list for the ushers;
  call them to confirm what they are doing,
  what time they need to arrive etc.
✧ Visit wedding and reception venue with the
  bride and groom to familiarise yourself with
  route, parking arrangements etc.
✧ Confirm order of speeches with bride and
  groom.
✧ Check the groom has the wedding ring.

2 WEEKS TO GO

✧ Finalise speech.

1 WEEK TO GO

✧ Attend wedding rehearsal and dinner.
✧ Collect order of ceremony sheets.
✧ Go with groom to collect hired clothing.
✧ Confirm arrangements for collecting
  buttonholes from bride.
✧ Check with groom that all honeymoon
  arrangements have been confirmed.
✧ Buy/collect together decorations for
  couple's getaway car.
✧ Give the bride and groom their gift and card
  from you.

1 DAY TO GO

✧ Charge up your mobile phone.
✧ Withdraw plenty of cash.
✧ Collect letters/cards from absent friends
  from bride's family.
✧ Check that the groom has the ring, knows
  where it is and that it is somewhere safe.

✧ HELP THE GROOM

Your main role in the run-up to the wedding is to support the groom and offer whatever help he needs. Stay in touch on a regular basis – this will not only help him, but it will help you be a better best man as you'll be fully aware of the arrangements. The week leading up to the big day is when your duties as right-hand man really come into their own. The groom will be nervous and forgetful. It's your job to allay his nerves and remind him of the things he has to do.

✧ TRANSPORT

It's not your job to arrange the transport for the wedding day, this is down to the groom, but you are responsible on the day for making sure that everyone gets to where they need to be and on time, so you need to be aware of the transport arrangements that have been made. Make sure that you know how everyone is travelling and who with. Make a note of the contact numbers for the companies/individuals involved and jot down the telephone numbers of a couple of local taxi firms just in case anything goes wrong and you need an alternative way to transport people.

✧ CLOTHING

This of course all depends on the formality and style of the wedding. The groom and his wife-to-be will have the ultimate say in this and, as best man, you should, quite literally, follow suit. I've been to some weddings where if the best man had worn a morning suit he would have looked quite ridiculous compared to everyone else. Equally I've been to some weddings where any guest not in a morning suit would have been very much frowned upon.

More and more grooms are choosing to dress themselves, their best man and all the ushers in matching suits. Whether the husband-to-be opts for lounge suits, black tie or morning dress, if it's smart looks, style and panache he's after then he can't do better than kit out all his closest friends in matching suits and ties. However, hiring five or six identical suits can be costly and it is usually the bride and groom who bear this cost. Some couples may be happy for the male members of the wedding party to wear suits they already own and then just hire matching ties or waistcoats.

If all of the guys are going to be dressed in hired or bought suits, it is safest if you all get fitted out together. It may seem like a fun idea to surprise everyone by hiring bright pink tails and a matching top hat, but rest assured, in the cold grey light of the wedding morning you'll suddenly realise that you're going to look pretty idiotic.

THE BEST (DRESSED) WOMAN

If you are the best woman it is very important to liaise with the bride, as well as the groom, about what you should wear. You will play a prominent role on the day and feature in many of the photographs, but remember that it is the bride who should be the most noticed female on the day, not you. So be sensitive to her feelings and discuss with her what you should wear. She may want your outfit to coordinate with the bridesmaid's.

HOW TO TIE A CRAVAT

1 Drape the cravat around your neck with
   the short end hanging to the left side of
   your chest.

2 Take the long end in your right hand and
   cross it over the short end.

3 Tuck the long end underneath the short
   end so it's now hanging on the right hand
   side of your chest.

4 Wrap the long end over the short end
   again so it's hanging to the left-hand side
   of your chest.

5 Bring the long end up through the loop
   that you have now created.

6 If you want to wear a self-tie cravat then
   just hang the long end down the front of
   your chest, tighten the knot and secure it
   all with a cravat pin.

7 But if you want a scrunchy tie then ignore
   the pin and simply tuck the long end
   through the loop you've created just like
   you would with a normal tie.

HOW TO TIE A BOW TIE

1 Drape the tie around your neck and cross one end over the other, making sure one end is slightly longer than the other.

2 Bring the long end up through the loop you've created.

3 Double the short end over itself to create the front base loop of the bow tie. Drop the long end down over this base loop.

4 While holding everything in place, double the long end back on itself to create the second loop of the bow tie. Then poke it through the loop behind the bow tie.

5 Adjust the bow tie by tugging at the ends and straightening the central knot. Don't worry if it's not perfectly symmetrical. All the best bow ties are ever so slightly askew. It proves that they're not clip-ons.

Oh, and talking of top hats – unless you're royalty (or a magician with a pet rabbit) then my advice would be, don't bother. They just look pompous. If the groom seems keen on hiring them then, as a good friend, you should do everything in your power to dissuade him from this fashion faux pas. You'll end up carrying it around all day and losing it; or else Auntie Joan will inadvertently sit on it. Don't forget that your get-up will be preserved for all time in the wedding photos.

If the clothing is being hired you should go with the groom the week before the wedding and help him to pick everything up and ensure that it finds its way to the correct member of the wedding party.

A wedding is one of the few occasions in your lifetime where you may be required to wear a cravat. (Unless of course you fancy yourself as something of a Regency Dandy). Chances are that none of the ushers or the groom will know how to tie one, so it's your job to make sure that you do. See page 42 to learn the easiest way to tie one properly.

At some weddings, especially ones that have an evening reception, you may be required to wear black tie. Clip-on or band bow ties are the worst. You have to go for a proper bow tie. See page 43 for how to tie it with style.

✧ YOUR GIFT

Amid all the chaos it's easy to forget that you too need to buy a wedding present and card for the happy couple. As best man your present should really be something special. You are honoured to be best friend to the groom and you ought to repay that honour by choosing a gift he and his wife will treasure.

The easiest option is to go for one of the more individual items on the wedding gift list (if the couple have one). But if you really want to make an impact, why not find out from them if there's something special that doesn't appear on the list? Or perhaps you can think of something yourself that will have special significance? Give your gift and card to the couple a few days before the wedding.

✧ ORGANISE THE USHERS

Even if your groom has appointed a chief usher you are ultimately in charge, so you should make sure they all know what they have to do. Although they are there to generally help out, the ushers have three main tasks:

1   To guide the guests into their seats at the wedding venue and hand out order of ceremony sheets. (See Seating the Guests, pages 56–58.)

2   To direct drivers into parking spaces at both the wedding and reception venues.

3   To provide guests with directions to the reception venue (See Direct People to the Reception, pages 62–63.)

Compile a list of their tasks and add any other relevant notes that they may find useful. If you think it will help, send them the list in advance so that they can take a look over it. Check that you still have all the ushers' mobile phone numbers in your phone from the stag party. Oh, and don't worry about the useless usher. You're bound to have one – every wedding does. Just be sure to give him a duty that he can't screw up too badly. Car parking isn't normally too taxing.

✧ THE RING

Yes, it's the ultimate marriage cliché: the lost wedding ring. More film footage and TV airtime is given to this particular scenario than any other part of the wedding. Insurance companies even offer policies now to cover this awful incident. And that's because it can and does happen. As best man you play a crucial part in ensuring it doesn't. First of all, check the groom has actually bought the ring well before the wedding day (three or four weeks is safe enough, and the bride usually has this task well in hand). See that he keeps it somewhere safe. The night before the wedding, make sure he doesn't go to bed without proving to you that he has it. Just to be on the safe side, keep a dress ring in your suit pocket for emergencies. A Hula Hoop will suffice if you're really desperate. (Apparently, even if it's edible it's still technically legal.)

Sometimes the best man is also required to keep hold of the bride's ring for the groom, although this duty is increasingly being handed over to the chief bridesmaid. Check with the bride whether she wants you to be in charge of both rings.

✧ ORDER OF CEREMONY AND WEDDING DAY SCHEDULE

An order of ceremony usually has the name of the bride and groom, date and the name of the wedding venue on the front. Inside it will list the different stages of the ceremony, as well as the words of any readings, hymns and prayers. Sometimes the best man, ushers, bridesmaids and page boys are credited too. If there is to be an order of ceremony sheet, it's often the duty of the best man to pick them up from the bride. Consult with the bride and arrange a convenient time with her, it's usually about a week before the wedding. Keep them in a safe place and obviously you need to remember to take them with you to the wedding venue. Depending on where and when the wedding is going to take place, you might be able to leave them at the wedding venue when you attend the rehearsal, but obviously don't do this unless you are absolutely sure that they won't be moved/thrown away etc.

A CAUTIONARY TALE

Do you remember the story of the newly-weds who booked a honeymoon to Sydney in Australia? They reserved the flights through a website, paid for the tickets and happily boarded the plane the day after their wedding. When the pilot announced that their flight was bound for Montreal in Canada, the hapless couple simply assumed that this was the first fuelling stop on the way to Australia. It wasn't until they had boarded their connecting flight – to Novia Scotia – that the penny finally dropped: there are two Sydneys – one on the east coast of Australia and one on the east coast of Canada. Needless to say, there were no opera houses or beach barbecues where they ended up.

There can be dozens of different instalments to a modern wedding that need to be organised with military precision, so most couples now also compile a wedding schedule with instructions for the best man, the ushers and the bridesmaids. You should arm yourself with several copies of this schedule as everyone involved will look to you to tell them what happens, where it happens and when. If you don't have a detailed schedule then chaos is bound to ensue. The bride and groom should print up a schedule a few days before the wedding. Help them to get this right.

✧ GROOM'S HONEYMOON PREPARATIONS

Bogged down in all the wedding preparations, the groom often forgets that things have to be organised for the honeymoon. This is one area where the bride may perhaps not be involved at all. It's worth checking with the groom that he hasn't overlooked any honeymoon preparations like tickets, passports, visas, inoculations, insurance, foreign currency etc.

✧ THE REHEARSAL

All the best public performances are preceded by a dress rehearsal. Weddings are no exception. This is a chance for everyone involved to iron out any last-minute problems and to ensure that everything goes swimmingly on the big day. The rehearsal is generally held one or two days before the wedding.

The main purpose of the rehearsal is to do a brief walk through of the actual ceremony so that all the members of the wedding party know exactly what they're supposed to do, where they have to stand, when to kneel etc., etc. Note that you're not required to wear your full wedding outfit to the rehearsal.

In addition to the run through, the rehearsal is an opportunity for you to familiarise yourself with the wedding venue and to check that the timing of the schedule and itinerary is realistic. The ushers should attend the rehearsal as well and this will give you the chance to confirm that they all know exactly what they're supposed to be doing. You'll also be able to reassure the groom, the bride and their families that you really are the right man for the job and that you're on top of things. Although if they still have any doubts at this late stage then perhaps you've been a little remiss in your earlier duties. This is the time for you to really shine.

Use this time to get to know the layout of the venue. Find out where the toilets are (I guarantee you'll be asked) and where everyone is

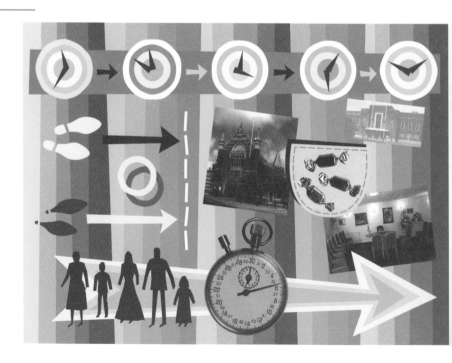

supposed to park their cars on the big day. Memorise exactly where everyone is supposed to sit, stand and speak. Above all, make certain that your opinion of what your duties are coincides exactly with the opinions of the groom, bride and their families. A good rule of thumb is simply to pay attention and do what you're told. At this late stage you will do no one any favours at all if you criticise the proceedings, however constructive you think your criticisms may be. Keep your suggestions to yourself and go with the flow. You have to see the wedding as a huge broth... with far too many cooks already trying to stir it. The list of these cooks is a long and distinguished one: the bride is on it; the groom may throw in a few wise words (but his voice will almost certainly be drowned out by the bride's); the bride's mother will have an opinion on everything; so might the groom's mother; then there's perhaps the wedding planner. People you won't find on this list are the father of the bride (even though he's probably foregoing his pension to pay for the reception), the father of the groom, and you, the best man. Just button your lip. Believe me, it'll be much better in the long run.

Whoever has been chosen to marry the couple – be it a vicar, a rabbi, a priest, a mullah, a registrar, a humanist or a druid, it's likely that he or she will want to run a pretty tight ship. No one wants the wedding from hell. No one wants to end up being featured on *You've Been Framed*, least of all the ceremony official. The rehearsal will probably be your first chance to meet this official. Pay attention and connect with him/her. This will help things run more smoothly at the main event. The rehearsal and the ceremony are not the places to clown around. That can wait until the reception.

There's a famous Hollywood adage which says "Never work with children or animals". Fortunately very few weddings feature our furry friends. But it's likely that if there are pageboys or bridesmaids at least one will be under the age of five. Little kids can be funny and little kids can be sweet. But a tantrum is never far away. Fortunately, as best man you won't be expected to deal with such a situation – unless of course the kid in question is yours. But you may be called upon to help out at some stage. Just be prepared. Make sure you know the kids' names, who their mums and dads are and most importantly, where they are. Keep a couple of sweets in your jacket pocket – they are the ultimate quick cure for tears and tantrums.

✦ THE REHEARSAL DINNER

The rehearsal dinner is an established tradition in the USA, and is one that is becoming increasingly popular in the UK. It used to be strictly an immediate family affair, plus perhaps the best man. But it is becoming more common for other family members, especially those who are travelling long distances to the wedding, plus ushers to be invited to attend.

By this stage all the hiccups will have been ironed out and the bride, groom and their families will be confident after the rehearsal. You too should have assuaged any worries you might have had. In any case, there's very little you can do this late in the day. Just relax, and look forward to the event you have been building up to.

Since you'll be making the main speech on the big day, you won't be expected to stand up and speak at the rehearsal dinner. But it's best to have a few words prepared just in case – even if it's just a few best wishes and a toast.

Oh, and don't overdo it on the booze. No one wants a best man with a hangover. Key decisions tend to go wrong. You should have done all your drinking at the stag party.

WHAT TO BRING ON THE DAY

Check off the items on this list:

☐	Suit	☐	Belt
☐	Waistcoat	☐	Handkerchief
☐	Shirt	☐	Umbrella
☐	Socks	☐	Cash
☐	Shoes	☐	Speech cue cards
☐	Cufflinks	☐	Letter/cards from absent friends
☐	Tie	☐	Order of ceremony sheets and wedding
☐	Underwear		schedule
		☐	Paperwork (licence etc)
		☐	Oops! Nearly forgot – the ring.

✧ MESSAGES FROM ABSENT FRIENDS

In the old days people who were unable to attend the wedding used to send telegrams. Nowadays it's more likely to be letters, cards or emails. Whatever the medium, it's your responsibility to read out messages from absent friends during your speech, so remember to pick these up from the bride's family the day before the wedding.

✧ THE NIGHT BEFORE THE BIG DAY

Depending on where the wedding is taking place and the arrangements that you've made, you may or may not be staying in the same place as the groom on the night before the wedding. If you're not staying in the same place and you're not going to see him, make sure you give him a call to check that he's OK and that he's set his alarm clock. Preferably two alarm clocks.

If you're staying in the same place, don't stay up talking half the night and don't drink too much. Use your time together productively and check that you have everything that you need for the big day. It will be less to worry about on the day itself.

CHAPTER 5

THE BIG DAY

Today is the day you really cannot afford to make any mistakes. Follow this guide and hopefully you won't. Weddings attract the unexpected, which is usually what makes them memorable, so be prepared to think on your feet. Lots of cash in your pocket and a fully-charged mobile phone should be weapons enough to see off most wedding day disasters. Give yourself the best chance to do the best job you possibly can. Go to bed early the night before, get a good night's sleep and rise early on the morning of the big day.

This timeline is for a mid-afternoon wedding. Use this as a guide to work out your own schedule for a wedding at a different time.

8AM:

✧ Wake up to your alarm clock. Today is not a day for a lie-in.

8.05AM:

✧ Wake up the groom. If you're not staying with him then phone him to wake him. (Increasingly, nowadays, best man and groom stay in the same hotel, or at the groom's place, the night before the wedding. It makes getting to the wedding venue on time a lot easier.)

8.10AM:

✧ Check the groom hasn't gone back to sleep.

8.15AM:

✧ Phone the chief usher to check he has everything under control.

8.20AM:

✧ Last-minute check of travel arrangements.

9AM:

✧ Check you have all the clothing, accessories, money and paperwork (licence or certificate of banns) you need. And for goodness sake remember the ring. (See What to Bring on the Day, page 51.)

MORNING:

✧ Collect buttonholes (and order of service sheets if you haven't collected them already) from the bride.

3 HOURS TO GO:

✧ Best man, groom and all the ushers meet up at the wedding venue. If you have to travel far to the wedding venue, always allow some extra journey time. Sod's Law dictates that traffic jams and engine problems are rife on wedding days. Check that you have the ring(s). Carry out any last minute checks.

2 HOURS TO GO:

✧ All proceed to the nearest pub for the ceremonial spot of pre-nuptial Dutch courage (see Pre-marital Drink, pages 55–56).

1 HOUR TO GO:

✧ Get to the venue and prepare to meet, greet and seat the guests as they arrive.

10 MINUTES TO GO:

✧ Check you have the ring(s). There's still time for an emergency ring if a real one has gone astray.

5 MINUTES TO GO:

✧ Take your position alongside the groom at the front of the venue.

THE BIG DAY

✧ KEEP THE GROOM CALM

Any sane man this close to getting married may start to get a little apprehensive at this stage. A mild panic may even have set in. You've got to be there to stave off these emotions. First of all you have to keep calm yourself. Imagine you are an air steward on an aeroplane and the groom is a passenger sitting on the row opposite your jump seat. If the engine starts to make funny noises and you display any apprehension, he will start to worry too. But if you keep cool under pressure, then hopefully so will he.

There may of course come a time when, despite your best intentions, the wings simply fall off the plane. This is when you become something of a counsellor for the groom. Keep reassuring him that everything will be okay. Get him to the ceremony on time and with as little stress as possible. You should be able to shield him from as many of the anxieties and tensions of the wedding day as you can so that he can focus on his main task: marrying his wife.

✧ TRANSPORT

It's likely you'll travel with the groom to the wedding venue on the morning of the big day. Better still, why not stay at his place the night before so that you can get him up and dressed in time? Aside from the stag night, this is the one time when you may have to mother the groom. It's possible his mind will be a jumble of nerves and his legs will be like jelly. You're his right-hand man and that may mean you'll have to help get him up and dressed, bundle him into the car and man-handle him to the wedding venue. Don't underestimate the effects that marriage stress can have on a man.

Transport is crucial at this stage. Do not even consider taking public transport to the wedding. Fellow travellers will cry with laughter when they spot you and the groom dressed up to the nines, stuck in traffic on a bus. You will cry with shame. Travel by car or taxi and plan to arrive at the wedding venue at least an hour and a half before everyone else. You'll need the spare time for any last minute problems and of course you'll want to meet all the ushers in the pub for a swift pint of Dutch courage prior to the ceremony (see Pre-marital Drink, pages 55–56). Always have a taxi firm on stand-by in case your car doesn't make it. You'll get some funny looks if you and the groom end up having to thumb a lift in your morning suits on the edge of the motorway.

✧ BUTTONHOLES

It's the bride who normally orders the buttonholes for her husband-to-be and his wedding party, along with the other numerous wedding flora. As best man it's your duty to get these buttonholes from her and onto your lapel and the lapels of the groom and ushers. Among all the other things you have to remember on the big day it may seem like just a trivial detail, but for the bride and her family it's important. Besides, if everyone is in morning suits then the buttonholes may be the only sign that you and the ushers are more than normal guests. You'll find that some guests will use the buttonholes to pick you out when they have questions to ask. The flowers are better than name tags and will be appreciated by the more short-sighted members of the wedding party.

✧ HELP THE BRIDE'S FAMILY

There are always last-minute emergencies and they normally involve something crucial like the cake or the marquee. Let the bride's parents know that, if needed, you are available to save the day.

I once heard about one poor best man who was roped into delivering a grandmother to the church on the wedding day because no one else had the time. The nonagenarian lived quite a distance from the ceremony and when the family phoned her on the morning of the big day she had completely forgotten about it. Best man was duly dispatched to pick her up, bundle her into his car and drive her posthaste to the church. He was hailed as a saviour by the bride and her family.

✧ PRE-MARITAL DRINK

This has become something of a tradition in recent years. Always try to build in enough time before the ceremony actually starts so that you and all the ushers can share a drink in a local pub with the groom. It is, after all, his final beverage as a free man and he will want to savour it with his closest friends.

It is also a chance to run over any last minute organisational details and to indulge in a bit of gallows humour at the groom's expense. In any case, which groom could even contemplate getting married on an empty stomach? Of all the types of courage he needs, Dutch courage is one of the most useful. Since no one, least of all the registrar or the bride, will appreciate slurred vows, limit the groom to just the one drink. In fact, that rule applies to everyone.

✧ THE CEREMONY
Seating the guests

The best man doesn't normally usher guests to their seats. His position is beside the groom. But he will have to ensure that the ushers know exactly what they have to do. At a formal wedding as the guests arrive ushers should hand them an order-of-ceremony sheet and direct them to the relevant side of the marriage venue. Traditionally, friends of the bride sit on the left-hand side of the venue and friends of the groom on the right-hand side. Nowadays, however, couples have often known each other for years before they get married and therefore have a lot of mutual friends. When this is the situation guests tend to mingle on both sides. Besides, it's often the case that the bride invites more people than the groom. If her father is paying for the wedding he may well have exercised his prerogative and invited a lot more of his own friends. If one side of the venue is full and the other empty, it can look a bit odd. Ushers should use their common sense and try to keep the guests balanced.

There are, however, certain key spots in the seating plan that need to be reserved. At a recent wedding I went to the ushers forgot to keep places free at the front of the church for the bride's family, all of whom arrived late. There were a few embarrassed looks as the mother of the bride and the ushers were forced to relocate some of the guests to the back of the church. Here's a tip: always fill the marriage venue from the back. Save the first few rows at the front for family members. The problem is that the ushers won't necessarily know who is family and who isn't. This is why they need to ask two questions to each guest on arrival: "Are you friends or family?"; "Bride or groom?". If someone answers "I'm friends with both bride and groom" then seat them on the groom's side. This will

SEATING PLAN

For a formal wedding here is the traditional seating plan:

LEFT	RIGHT
Bride's parents	Groom and best man
Bride's family and bridesmaids	Groom's parents
Bride's other relatives	Groom's close family
	Groom's other relatives
Bride's friends	Groom's friends
Ushers	Ushers

help balance numbers if the bride has invited more guests.

At very formal weddings ushers may be expected to offer their arms to female guests and escort them to their seats. If the female guest is accompanied by a man then he would follow along behind. Some women will enjoy this courtesy while others may feel uncomfortable at all the fuss. As the guests continue to arrive the ushers will quickly learn to gauge the situation.

Ushers

Here are a few tips to give to your ushers:

- At all times act courteously and speak calmly with clear instructions.
- Try to seat old and vulnerable guests in the coolest part of the building. A summer wedding party with 150 people in formal dress will soon heat up a venue to an uncomfortable level. You don't want guests to snore during the ceremony.
- If loads of guests arrive at the same time speed up the proceedings by allowing them to seat themselves.
- You don't need to accompany every female guest to her seat. Concentrate on the older ones and ones who arrive alone. Don't walk too fast – stiletto heels tend to get stuck in church floor grates.
- After the ceremony ushers should check the wedding venue for lost property. Ladies' hats in particular tend to go astray. (I remember being an usher at one wedding where someone had left a wedding gift under one of the church pews.)

Waiting with the groom

Be prepared to wait for quite a while for the bride to arrive. During this time you should be giving the groom all the moral support he needs. This could well be his most vulnerable hour, the period when he finds himself more nervous than he has ever been since he first proposed.

You won't have to stand at the front of the wedding venue with him for the entire period that you are waiting for the bride. Ushers should have been appointed to act as lookouts so that they can give you the signal the moment the bride arrives. Normally when you get

ON CEREMONY

You could be standing up for quite a while before and during the ceremony, and after the bride and groom you will be the next focus of everyone's attention. Here are a few tips on how to get through the ceremony with grace:

1 Don't lock your knees when standing for a long time. It will restrict blood flow to your lower legs and may cause you to topple.

2 Stand up straight and keep still. Every now and then subtly shift your weight from one foot to the other. This prevents fainting too.

3 No nail biting or nose picking, no matter how nervous you are. Even if there is no videographer, there will always be a guest lurking somewhere with a camcorder.

4 Avoid chewing gum. Little mints are much more subtle.

5 Smile. Even if your nerves are shot to pieces on the inside, this should be a happy day for you too.

6 However casual the ceremony, don't be tempted to put your hands in your pockets. By your side or behind you are the only options.

7 The bride and groom should be your main focus of attention so that you play your part in the ceremony at the right time. Don't look around for friends or try to attract their attention. There'll be plenty of time for socialising at the reception.

this signal, you and the groom will take your positions at the front of the venue, opposite the clergyman or the registrar, in readiness for the bride and her father.

This is often when the extreme anxiety kicks in. A groom who has up until now been cool, calm and collected, may suddenly realise the gravity of his situation, just as the bride makes her entrance. As best man, you've got to hold it all together for yourself and for your groom. If you need to mutter reassuring words under your breath to him then don't be afraid to do so. You will quite literally be his right-hand man, standing just to his right side. Do whatever is required to keep him focused and calm: act casual, whisper kind words, or even try to take his mind off the seriousness of the occasion if you need to. Just keep him cool. How many *You've Been Framed* clips have you seen where the groom faints and keels over at the crucial moment? It happens so often that a lot of wedding officials keep smelling salts in their

PRACTICAL JOKE

Just like the humiliation of the groom on the stag do, wedding day practical jokes are also a nuptial tradition. What you mustn't do, however, is overdo the joke and throw the bride and groom off course or do anything to spoil their day. For most of the early part of the day they will be vulnerable souls. You'll know best how the couple will react. It's up to you to gauge whether a joke will be appreciated.

A classic trick which the best man can play is to write a message in white paint on the soles of the groom's wedding shoes, so that it's visible to the whole congregation when he kneels at the altar. 'Help' on the left sole and 'me!' on the right sole tends to work quite well.

Oh, and don't think that just because it's not you getting married that you won't be subject to a few practical jokes yourself. A friend of mine attended a Catholic wedding where the bride, groom and all the ushers had to kneel together at the altar during the ceremony. Various messages like 'I'm next', 'You think he's nervous?' and 'Help me too!' had been painted on the soles of the shoes of the best man and his ushers.

pockets. They claim that they're required more for grooms than for brides.

The ring

It's your job to safeguard the ring (or the rings, if you're also looking after the groom's ring from the bride) until the crucial moment. Keep it in your front pocket. Don't put it on your own finger. Imagine the embarrassment if, because of nerves and heat, your fingers swell up and you can't get the ring off again. You do not want to end up mutating from best man into groom do you?

Signing the register

It's normal for just the parents, the groom and the bride to sign the register. But occasionally the best man and chief bridesmaid are asked to do this. Don't worry, it's very self-explanatory.

The procession

At a church wedding it's traditional for the best man to accompany the bridesmaids out of the church after the bride and groom. All eyes will be on you and the rest of the wedding party and the only time you'll have more cameras pointed at you is if one day you enter court on a murder charge. So make the most of it. Walk slowly and calmly, with perhaps a bridesmaid on each arm. Enjoy the attention and keep smiling.

If the bride's dress gets tangled, just remember it's not your job to fix it. This is the exclusive domain of the chief bridesmaid. Besides, wedding dresses are often huge, rambling affairs. You think you're being helpful but you'll only end up making things worse.

Wedding fee
This is normally the domain of the father of the bride and should have been settled well beforehand. But if payment has been overlooked you may be required to cover costs, at least temporarily. Before the wedding day, check diplomatically with the bride and groom as to who is financially responsible.

Confetti
Certain venues can be a bit sniffy about confetti, especially if it's not the variety that birds can eat. You may be asked to make an announcement on the subject before the ceremony starts.

It's a good idea for you to provide some confetti of your own. It looks great in the photographs and if you have several packets on your person you can collude with the photographer and time your bombardment to perfection.

The tradition of throwing confetti dates back to pre-Christian times when guests showered the newly-weds with grain to symbolize fertility.

Help the photographer
The wedding photographer never knows the names of everyone he's supposed to be capturing on film; unless he's a very old family friend, in which case his photos risk being blurred and shaky.

Professional photographers need help with their task and they always look to the best man for assistance. It's a good idea if you and the snapper have a list of what shots are required. Along with

THE NO-SHOW GROOM

What should you do if the groom fails to turn up?! This is another one of those Hollywood nightmare scenarios: the groom who loses his nerve at the last minute and fails to turn up for the wedding ceremony. The good news is that, as best man, unlike in the olden days, you are no longer obliged to marry the bride in his place. The bad news is that you now have no rest until you have found him. The responsibility is on your shoulders.

Get things organised quickly. Rally together a search party, using only people from the groom's side of the family. If members of the bride's family find him who knows what might happen?

Check the obvious places: his family home; his ex-girlfriend's place; the nearest airport; the pub; a high cliff. If you do find him then be sure to treat him with kid gloves. By this stage he will be a very fragile animal indeed. Thoughts of wedded bliss will be far from his mind. Instead he'll be considering emigration.

If he really has made up his mind and you can't talk him into going ahead with marriage, then sorry, but it's your job to break it to the bride and her family. By this time their extreme rage will have developed into a desire for his blood. Since the groom is about to leave the country, it's you who will be next in the firing line. The father of the bride will be especially belligerent. His beloved daughter has just been jilted at the altar; he has been shown up in front of all his friends; and now he's got a hefty bill for a reception that no one's going to attend. In the absence of the groom, he will turn his aggression on you instead. Apologise profusely and sympathise with his situation. Don't reveal the groom's whereabouts and don't ask if he's got a job lot of champagne he wants to sell to you. Consider boarding that plane to Brazil along with the groom.

the ushers you can then rally all the relevant people together and make sure the right heads are in the right photos. People will be desperate to get to the reception and get started on the champagne, so keep the photo session as painless as possible.

Most of the photos will be very formal. Your bride and groom will be grateful if you and the ushers arrange some fun shots towards the end of the session. The bride lying across the arms of the groom, best man and all the ushers is a favourite.

Direct people to the reception

A loud voice and an assertive manner are needed for this duty. The bride and groom will be falling over each other in post-nuptial bliss, so it's up to you to make certain that all the guests know exactly how to get to the reception.

Out of 150-odd guests there are sure to be some who can't quite make the transition from ceremony to reception. The best man is their only hope of reaching the champagne and therefore they'll latch onto you for directions.

If you have enough ushers you can position them at key turning points on the route. Arms outstretched, dressed in morning suits and adorned with buttonhole flowers, they will be more obvious than any number of signposts.

✧ THE RECEPTION
The receiving line

The receiving line is the first port of call for all the guests once they arrive at the reception. Not every wedding has one but when they do it's a chance for guests to officially meet and congratulate the bride, groom and their parents.

The traditional order of a receiving line is the bride's mother and father, the groom's parents, and the bride and groom. It's unlikely you'll be asked to actually stand in the line, but if you are you should stand at the end with the chief bridesmaid. You'll actually be more useful directing the guests once they arrive at the reception. Guide them first to the receiving line. In the absence of one of these send them straight for the trays of bubbly. They won't need much encouragement for the latter.

Dinner seating arrangements

At a lot of weddings the best man sits at the top table with the bride, groom and their families. Chances are you'll be in such demand that you won't have time to enjoy the wine before the speeches. Don't be tempted, though. One glass is okay, but any more and you'll seriously risk messing up the speech.

Drunken guests

By no means is the best man expected to act as doorman, but you may be called upon to help if guests get out of hand. Alcohol affects different people in different ways and there are always a couple of guests who imbibe too much. If someone really is causing an embarrassment then you ought to try to remove them from the reception until they have sobered up a bit. A good way of doing this is to get one of the staff to tell the offending person that he (and yes it is normally a 'he') has a phone call in the main house/hotel reception. Once he has stumbled away from the reception you can collar him and politely explain that he needs to sober up. This will avoid a scene in front of all the other guests.

I heard of one particular wedding where the bride had invited one of her ex-boyfriends. Under normal circumstances this would have been okay. Unfortunately, after many glasses of champagne, circumstances were anything but normal. The ex-boyfriend got totally drunk and decided to try to reignite his relationship with the bride... much to the chagrin of her new husband. It was left to the best man to step in and sort things out. With supreme tact worthy of a Middle-Eastern diplomat he managed to guide the ex-boyfriend out of the marquee, sober him up a bit with lots of strong black coffee and finally make him see the error of his ways.

Master of ceremonies

If it's a very formal wedding there may be a toastmaster, in which case you only have to worry about your own speech. But at some weddings you may be called upon to do a bit of MC-ing. Normally this just involves making an announcement when dinner is served, ensuring that the microphone works and that the speeches take place in the correct order. More and more wedding speeches are being scheduled before the guests sit down for dinner, but conventionally they take place after dessert when the guests are drinking their coffee.

Once you and the other speakers are ready to strut your stuff, stand up and jingle a spoon in a wine glass to get everyone's attention. Introduce the first speaker. Traditionally the father or close friend of the bride opens up proceedings. His job is to thank all the guests for coming and to welcome his new son-in-law into the family. He will also reveal a few embarrassing anecdotes about the bride's early life before proposing a toast to the newly-weds.

Now it's the turn of the groom. His job is easy since the main function of his speech is to thank everyone for making the wedding day possible. This must include both sets of parents and all the guests, and possibly even the caterers and florists etc. He should then wax lyrical about the bridesmaids and of course his beautiful new wife.

Now it's crunch time. The moment of truth. Your opportunity to really shine. The best man's speech (see Part Two, pages 78–119).

CHAPTER 6

FINAL DUTIES

A lot of best men make the mistake of believing that once they have punctuated their speech with the final toast then their duties are complete. Not quite. You're still expected to a certain extent to be a gracious party host and to ensure everyone enjoys a great reception. You also ought to take charge of getting the couple safely away on their honeymoon. Don't miss this chance to indulge in the classic wedding tradition of decorating the honeymooners' car.

✧ PARTY HOST

As best man, you are, in a way, one of the hosts of the wedding reception. Once you've delivered your speech it's then part of your job to keep the party going. You'll certainly be expected to dance with the chief bridesmaid, to get up on the dancefloor early and to encourage everyone else to dance. You may need to give direction to the band or the DJ. You have a responsibility for ensuring that everyone has a good time. Saying that, don't deny yourself a few drinks. By this stage you will very much deserve them.

✧ GETTING THE COUPLE AWAY

Long gone are the days when the married couple would depart from the reception after dinner, leaving their guests to enjoy the party without them. Nowadays the bride and groom are expected to be the life and soul of the party all the way until the end of the evening. With so many big weddings taking place in marquees, they may even be hosting a lunch the following day.

But eventually the time will come when they head off on their

WHY DO WE TIE THINGS TO THE COUPLE'S CAR?

This tradition harks all the way back to ancient Egypt. When Egyptian traders clinched a deal they used to exchange sandals with one another as a sign that goods had been transferred from one person to another. When a girl married her new husband, the bride's father would give the groom his sandals, to signify that his daughter was now his property. (There was of course no such thing as sexual equality in ancient times.)

The Romans took the tradition one step further and used to throw shoes over the happy couple at the end of the wedding ceremony. This was gradually modified over the centuries until it became customary to tie shoes to the back of the wedding carriage, and later the motor car, as the newly-weds drove away.

In the final evolution of the tradition shoes were replaced with tin cans.

honeymoon. Your last duty as best man is to see that their final transition into married life goes smoothly. Help them get their honeymoon bags packed into the car. Take charge of any clothing the groom may have hired and ensure it gets back to the hire shop. And promise the newly-weds that you will see any presents left over from the wedding safely home. If you live nearby offer to take care of their house while they are away – taking in the post etc. It would be a generous touch to get some basic supplies in and pop a bottle of champagne in the fridge for when they get back home.

Decorate the car

As best man, you should help decorate their car. The old but very effective cliché is to tie tin cans to the rear bumper or spray 'Just Married' across the rear windscreen. Festering kippers under the bonnet used to be an old favourite, too. A safer option, though, is to tie streamers to the wing mirrors and balloons to the aerial.

Bride and groom will love the attention as they drive off from the reception knowing that everyone they pass on the road will know they are newly-weds. It's one of the more romantic episodes in a typical wedding day – why do you think it has featured in so many films over the years? Oh, and it makes for great photos, too. But remember – it's not funny to interfere with the mechanics of the car. Bride and groom may have a plane to catch.

If the couple are staying the night locally before embarking on their honeymoon, a hotel room practical joke may be in order. This may range from the safe option of confetti in the bedclothes to the slightly more risky cling film stretched over the toilet seat. Again, use your judgement as to whether a joke will go down well or not. Once you've waved them off, pour yourself a well-earned drink.

At the end of the day

Before you can call it day, be sure to offer your help to the bride's and groom's parents – they may need assistance clearing up, loading the car etc.

Congratulations,
you have succeeded in your role as best man.

CHAPTER 7

WEDDING CUSTOMS

Every nation, culture and religion has its own particular take on the wedding ceremony and party afterwards. Civil weddings last just a few minutes while Catholic ceremonies can go on for several hours. In India you're lucky to get the whole thing over in less than a week. In today's multicultural society you may well be asked to be best man at a wedding where the customs are totally unfamiliar to you.

The bride and groom may be of different nationalities or from different faiths and wish to combine elements of both. The bride and groom will brief you as to your duties and tell you everything you need to know. You should respect any traditions that are called for. This chapter also covers same-sex and double-weddings.

✧ CATHOLIC WEDDINGS

There are two types of Roman Catholic wedding: a simple ceremony and a full nuptial mass. For the latter, which lasts longer since it includes holy communion, bride and groom must both be Catholic. As well as a ring, the groom gives gold and silver to his bride as a symbol of his worldly goods.

✧ JEWISH WEDDINGS

The ceremony takes place in a synagogue, normally underneath a canopy decorated with flowers. If it's Orthodox, male and female guests sit on opposite sides and cover their heads. After the vows have been exchanged the couple sip wine from the same glass and the groom will then break the glass under the heel of his shoe. As best man you will probably be asked to sign as a witness to the licence. Also, a point to note is that it is not traditional for the best man to make a speech at a Jewish wedding.

✧ MUSLIM WEDDINGS

Many Muslims hold a wedding over several days. But the actual ritual is a fairly simple affair.

The bride and groom are in separate rooms where they may or may not be able to see one other, depending on how conservative the families are. An officiant, familiar with Islamic law, heads to each room separately and asks both the bride and groom if they consent to the marriage. The couple then signs the marriage contract while witnesses look on. Finally the officiant brings the bride and groom together and pronounces them husband and wife.

Before and after the actual marriage there are many different traditional ceremonies, depending on which Muslim country the couple lives in.

Having a best man is not a custom at a traditional Muslim wedding. On the wedding day a procession of the groom's friends and family accompany him to the wedding venue.

✧ CIVIL WEDDINGS

If this is held in a registry office it will be a very simple affair with just a few guests. If it is held in a larger licensed venue like a civic hall or a historic building then it could have all the pomp of a religious wedding, just without the religious language.

✧ DOUBLE WEDDINGS

Not surprisingly, very few brides are willing to share the limelight with another bride on their special day. That's why double weddings would normally only feature siblings, where the guests are mostly mutual too.

Each groom will have his own best man and each best man will act pretty much the same as if it was a single wedding. If you find yourself best man at a double wedding it's crucial you meet up with your counterpart well before the ceremony to share notes.

In the case of two sisters it's traditional for the eldest bride and her bridesmaids to walk down the aisle first. If the brides aren't sisters then the bride with the elder groom normally takes precedence.

✧ GAY WEDDINGS

A lot of Western countries are starting to relax the laws on same sex marriages. Since traditionally there are no set procedures for gay weddings, couples can come up with their own ideas. When two men are tying the knot you'd expect a best man and when there are two women getting married you'd expect a best woman. There are no hard and fast rules governing this, however. Some gay weddings feature two best men or women, with each person in the couple having chosen someone. Otherwise the ceremony pretty much follows the conventions of a civil wedding. There are very few religions around the world yet progressive enough to allow gay weddings in their churches.

✧ WEDDING TRADITIONS

The world is a small place, so you may find yourself the best man at a wedding in a foreign country. Every country has its own quirky wedding traditions. Here are some of the more interesting ones.

Armenia

At a traditional Armenian church wedding the best man is called the 'brother of the cross'. During the reception the guests throw coins at the bride.

China

Chinese brides will often change their wedding dress at least three times during the day.

Croatia

Wedding guests walk three times around a well and then throw apples into it. This symbolises the fertility of the newly-weds.

Cyprus

Guests pin money to the bride and groom during the first dance.

Czech Republic

Before the ceremony a baby is placed on the couple's bed to encourage fertility.

Denmark

Guests will cut the groom's tie and socks with scissors.

Estonia

The Estonians have a tradition for predicting which bachelor guest will be the next to get married. They blindfold the groom and whichever head he places his top hat on will be the next to marry.

Finland

The bride's mother-in-law puts a plate on the bride's head at the start of the wedding dance. When the plate falls the number of broken pieces represent how many children the couple will have.

Greece
Along with the priest, the best man is in charge of the ceremony. He places gold crowns or wreaths made of orange blossoms on the head of the bride and groom. Plates are smashed on the floor during the reception.

Hungary
If male guests dance with the bride and give her coins then she kisses them in return.

India
The day before the ceremony the bride will have her hands and feet decorated with henna paint.

Indonesia
Everyone who even vaguely knows the bride or groom is invited to an Indonesian wedding. There can often be thousands of guests.

Iran
After the ceremony the bride and groom will have shavings of sugar dropped onto their heads.

Japan
The bride wears a hood on her kimono to hide what are called her 'horns of jealousy'.

Korea
The groom's father throws red dates at the bride in order to help her become fertile.

Latvia
The ushers often pretend to kidnap the bride at a Latvian wedding. The groom then has to buy a round of drinks to win her back.

Malaysia
Each guest receives a hard-boiled egg which symbolises the fertility of the married couple.

Morocco
After the wedding the bride walks around her new house three times before she crosses the threshold.

Norway
Whenever the groom leaves the room during the reception, all the single men queue up to kiss the bride in his absence. It also works the other way; when the bride leaves all the single women kiss the groom.

Pakistan
Weddings last four days with the actual ceremony on the third day.

Poland
It is considered lucky if a Polish bride drinks from a ceremonial glass of wine without spilling a drop.

Russia
After the toasts, guests throw their champagne glasses on the floor. It's good luck if they break.

Sudan
After the wedding the newly-weds break an egg before entering their new home.

Sweden
Just before the bride gets married her parents give her a silver and gold coin. She puts one of each in each shoe.

Thailand
Bride, groom and guests dip their hands in a conch shell full of water for good luck.

Tibet
Bride and groom are given ceremonial scarves to wear around their necks. Sometimes there are so many that they can't see from beneath them.

PART TWO

THE SPEECH

CHAPTER 8

BASIC STRUCTURE

This is the moment you've really been preparing for. It's the one best man's duty that you will most be remembered for. And this is very probably the part of the day you have most been dreading. Fear not, however. This section gives you a basic speech structure that you can either follow exactly, or adapt and change as you see fit.

My brother has been best man three times. The first time he was so nervous about his speech he used to wake up in the middle of the night with nightmares. And that was three months before the big day. The second time he was a bit more relaxed. He'd been through it once before and knew what to expect. The third time it was a breeze. Without any doubt, the key to making a great speech is preparation.

Whatever you do and however accustomed you are to public speaking do NOT try to wing it on the day. You're going to be standing up in front of possibly 150 or more people, many of them strangers. You're probably going to be wearing a hot, formal suit. You're expected to be courteous, grateful, full of praise and funny. On the outside you've got to look smart, confident and in control. However, it's very likely that on the inside your nerves will be shot to pieces.

There are three stages to any great speech: writing, practising and delivering. Even if you're the most nervous public speaker in the world, provided you take heed of the following advice, I can guarantee you'll be able to present a heartfelt and witty speech which all the guests and especially the bride and groom are bound to remember – for all the right reasons, that is. Traditionally the father of the bride speaks first, followed by the groom, and then it's your turn.

✧ HOW THE SPEECH SHOULD RUN

You're free to deliver the key elements of your speech in any order you like. But there should be a logical progression to what you say. Here is a fail-safe structure.

1   Great opening line
    Get things going with an unforgettable opening line. Make your audience laugh and they'll be on your side right from the start (see Great Opening Lines, pages 87–90).

2   Thanks and a joke
    Thank both the father of the bride and the groom for their speeches. Sound sincere when you do this, even if one of the speeches was a stinker.

As best man, it's not your official duty to thank the parents of the bride and all the other contributors who helped with the wedding. However, just to be on the safe side, why not throw in a few well meant words of gratitude?

Now make a joke about how the groom is soon to have his character well and truly assassinated. There's nothing wrong with instilling a bit of fear in him. You want the guests to be full of anticipation and the groom to be full of dread about what you are about to reveal.

3   Reply on behalf of the bridesmaids
Your traditional role as best man is to reply to the groom on behalf of all the bridesmaids. You don't need to be too formal about this, but you must remind everyone how beautiful they all look. They have spent hours in front of the mirror and have endured weeks of dress-fittings. A throwaway remark about how nice they look isn't enough. You've really got to wax lyrical about their beauty. Try to sound genuine rather than sycophantic. Also give the younger members of the bridal party a mention too.

4   Congratulate the newly-weds
Give your congratulations to the newly-weds. As with so much of the best man's speech there's a fine line between sounding sincere and cheesy. You don't need to employ nauseating lovey-dovey language. However professionally you deliver cheesy words, they will always sound cheesy. It's far better to come up with a few simple, well-meant tidings.

Look at the couple fondly as you congratulate them. They and everyone else will notice the expression in your face as you do this and realise the message is coming from your heart. And remember to tell them how honoured you are to have been chosen as best man.

If you do end up sounding too schmaltzy you can always try ending your congratulations with a few marriage witticisms:

> "[Bride], treat him just like a pet dog – plenty of exercise, lots of affection, three meals a day and a loose lead."

"[Groom], make sure you cuddle and kiss her daily. And if her daily won't agree to it, try the au pair!"

5   Compliment the bride

Although compliments to the bride are not an official part of your speech duty, a line about how beautiful the bride looks will always be appreciated. This will also encourage the guests who will clap and cheer in support after you say it.

6   The groom's in safe hands

Now you can talk about how the groom is in very safe hands with his new bride. It's an opportunity for you to describe to everyone how utterly useless the groom is around the house and at looking after himself. Try the following:

"Around the house, [groom] is like God Himself. He's never seen, he thinks he's the holy of holies and if he even so much as lifts a finger it's considered a bloody miracle."

"[Groom] is extremely responsible indeed. If anything ever goes wrong you can be sure that it's him who's responsible."

But be sure it's only the groom you mock. Whatever you do, don't take the mickey out of the bride.

7   Mock the groom
At this juncture you can go on the offensive. This is your chance to really make fun of the groom and in the process make your audience laugh. However, the humour should always be affectionate and playful.

Perhaps pick on a particular aspect of the groom's character and expose it for the benefit of everyone present. (See Subjects to Avoid, pages 90–92 and Safe Joke Material page 93.)

If the groom is renowned for being forgetful:

"[Groom] doesn't know the meaning of the word forgetful. Mind you, there are loads of words he doesn't know the meaning of."

If the groom's a bit slow on the uptake:

"In all the many years I've known [groom], no one has ever questioned his intelligence. In fact, come to think of it, I don't think I've ever heard anyone even mention it."

If the groom is bad at DIY:

"[Groom] has been described as awkward, bumbling and cack-handed. Let's face it – a mother should know these things."

If the groom is lazy:

"[Groom] is a very lucky man. His job allows him to work eight hours and sleep eight hours. Unfortunately they tend to be the same eight hours."

8   Praise the groom
Always balance these jokes by following them with some serious and poignant stuff. Remember you're there to praise the groom as well as ridicule him in front of family and friends. You are,

after all, his best man. Tell everyone what a great friend he is to you and remind everyone what a terrific bloke he is.

If you're worried it's all starting to sound a bit cheesy you can always follow it with a playful put-down.

Try this:

"Just take a look at the groom. What a wonderful man he is. [Pause.] Maybe we can cryogenically freeze him until scientists find a cure."

Or:

"[Groom's] so unique that it's almost impossible to forget him. But, believe me, it's well worth the effort."

9 Anecdotes

Now it's time for all the anecdotes and funny stories you have prepared (see Ideas, pages 94–95). The guests will love being entertained by the antics, capers and various scrapes that the groom has been involved in over the years. Use these tales to paint a picture of his character and get lots of laughs from the guests. Embellishment and exaggeration is perfectly acceptable; to be expected even.

One thing you must be sure not to do is alienate your listeners with in-jokes and obscure stories that they can't relate to. A 10-minute story hinting at events which took place on the stag do may have all the ushers in stitches, but the rest of the wedding guests won't understand and won't be interested. Try to keep it relevant to everyone if you can. And don't be too cruel to the groom (see Subjects to Avoid, pages 90–92).

10 Heartfelt wishes

In your efforts to make everyone laugh, don't forget that your speech should include some emotional stuff. If you feel you may have overdone the ridiculing then you can always throw in something about how lucky the groom is and what a perfect couple the newly-weds are. By alternating funny stuff with heartfelt stuff you ensure that your speech remains balanced.

11 Messages from absentees

Now's the time to read out any messages from guests who couldn't make it to the wedding. If there are no absentees, why not include a few fabricated messages, just for a laugh?

"Dear [groom],
We'd like to take this opportunity on your wedding day to give
you and your new bride our very best wishes for your future life
together. By the way, do you wish to renew your subscription?
Yours sincerely,
Playboy magazine."

12 Quotation or poem

Start to wrap up your speech with a quotation or a poem. But keep it short. As best man, your speech will be the third one of the day. Deliver a 10-minute poem and some of your guests will nod off. Try not to use anything too sentimental. There are hundreds of quotations and poems to choose from (see pages 95–102 for a selection of quotations and pages 123–124 for further sources.)

13 Toast

Finish your speech with a toast (see pages 103–105 for some examples). At this stage of the speeches everyone will be dying to nip to the toilet and then get to the bar. Your toast will be a recognisable punctuation point. Always end it with a simple phrase that everyone can repeat together, like "The bride and groom!"

CHAPTER 9

WRITING
THE SPEECH

So, you have a basic structure to work to. Start composing your speech months, not days before the wedding. That's not to say it will take you months to write. It's likely you'll be able to sit down one evening and put all the salient points on paper (or preferably computer) within a couple of hours. If you do this early enough then you'll have lots of time to add material, fine-tune your words and practise your actual delivery.

✧ SPEECH LENGTH

Depending on the formality of the wedding, most best men's speeches run for between 7 and 12 minutes. If it's a 1,000-guest royal wedding you're best man for then you can make it longer; if it's family and a couple of friends in the village hall then you'd probably want to make it shorter. Check with the groom and the father of the bride as to how long they are planning to speak for. Your speech should be the longest of the three, but not by a disproportionate amount. You're not showboating, you're communicating.

✧ PUTTING PEN TO PAPER

If possible, the best thing to do is to type your speech on a computer. That way you can amend and add to it over the weeks in the run-up to the wedding. Jot down the bare bones and then gradually flesh it out until you have it in full. This is when you need to make a decision as to how you're going to deliver your speech – are you going to read it word for word or use cue cards? (See pages 107 and 115).

If you're not confident that you can remember your speech just from notes or bullet points then you can always separate the fully-written speech into small sections, print it out and then glue each section to a separate cue card. If you're going to read your speech this is the best way to prepare it as it avoids you holding several sheets of flimsy paper.

If you're going to deliver your speech using notes or bullet points you will need to have virtually memorised it (see page 107). When you have memorised it edit your speech document (keeping a copy of the original, just in case) so that you are left with the key points and the best lines. Make the type larger than you would for a normal letter or document. Print the bullet points out onto sheets of paper, cut them up and glue a few bullet points to each cue card. Number the cards, then punch a hole in the top left corner and group the cards together using a treasury tag. This way if you drop your cards you can pick them up and carry on rather than scrabbling around trying to get them back in order.

✧ GREAT OPENING LINES

They say that first impressions last. It's the same with speeches. Seasoned wedding-goers will tell you how important it is for the best man to get the guests on his side from the very start. To do this you need to open your speech with a killer opening line. It doesn't necessarily have to be hilarious and it doesn't have to be entirely original (none of those listed below are), but try to avoid clichés and jokes that may not appeal to everyone present.

1 *"Apparently there are four crucial duties for a best man:*

One: Help the groom get dressed. He really should know how to do that by now.

Two: Make sure he has a pee before he gets married. Look, I don't mind sending him to the toilet, but I'm not willing to check he actually has a pee.

Three: Ensure the groom's face and hair are in order. Well, if God couldn't get it right the first time then I've got no hope.

Finally: Make a speech to the bride and groom. Now, I was under the naive impression that this meant just the bride and groom. You know, maybe just us three in the vestry, having a chat and a cup of tea. So you can imagine how worried I was when I found out I actually had to do it in front of 100 people."

2 [If the groom's paying for the wedding.] *"Typical. It's the first time [groom's] ever bought me dinner and I was so nervous about the speech that I couldn't eat it."*

3 *"Ladies and gentlemen... the groom gave me a short list of topics I wasn't allowed to cover in the speech.* [Remove a large wad of cue cards from your breast pocket and throw them away behind you.] *There goes most of my speech then. Feel reassured now, [groom]?"*

4 *"Ladies and gentlemen. This is the moment you've all been waiting for.* [Pause]. *And there it goes."*

5 *"I don't mind telling you I'm a little nervous. This isn't the first time today I've stood up from a warm seat with a piece of paper in my hand."*

6 *"Unaccustomed as I am to pubic spanking... Oops!"*

7 *"I just realised, while [father of the bride's] and [groom] were speaking before me, how much they have in common. After all, it's the first time in 25 years that [father of the bride] has been able to speak for more than five minutes without interruption from the women in his family, and it'll be the last time in 25 years that [groom] gets to do the same."*

8 *"Over the years I've been like a mother to [groom]. I've watched him drink from the bottle; I've seen him stagger around completely naked; I've seen him trying to crawl; I've had to dress him. I've had to undress him. And God knows how many times I've cleaned up after him. I've even had to help him walk."*

9 *"Fornication....Uh, sorry ...* [Say clearly and slowly] *"FOR AN OCCASION such as this I was dreading making the speech. That was until I found out exactly what I was supposed to say as best man. I discovered that once I'd hacksawed through [groom's] handcuffs the morning after the stag night, and once I'd handed [groom] the ring before today's service, all that was left was a five minute speech in which I was to absolutely demolish [groom's] character. Never one to shun my duties, here goes..."*

10 *"Marriage is a wonderful thing. Marriage will teach [groom] loyalty, self restraint and control. It will develop in him a sense of fair play and many other qualities he wouldn't need if he had stayed single."*

11 [For best men who wear glasses.] *"On the request of [groom], I have tried to memorise my speech. My memory's not as good as it used to be, so forgive me if I occasionally consult my notes. I did ask for an auto-cue, but apparently the wedding budget doesn't stretch that far.* [Putting on glasses] *Neither does my eyesight."*

12 *"Ladies and gentlemen, I'm only going to speak for a couple of minutes because of my throat. If I go on too long, [bride] says she'll cut it."*

13 *"If there's anybody here this afternoon who feels slightly nervous, it's probably because you just got married to [groom]."*

14 *"In making this speech I feel like one of Elizabeth Taylor's husbands. There have been so many before. The problem is how to make it interesting."*

15 *"You know it's great to be at a normal wedding for once. Last week I went to a wedding where two aerials got married. The ceremony was dreadful, but the reception was great!"*

16 *"Six months ago when [groom] asked me to be his best man I decided to do a bit of research. All the books told me there are three crucial stages to the ceremony:*

1 The aisle – it's the longest walk you'll ever take.

2 The altar – the place where two become one.

3 The hymn – A choral celebration of the marriage.

I think [bride] may have read the same books as me because as she took her place beside [groom] today, I swear I heard her whispering 'Aisle Altar Hymn, Aisle Altar Hymn'."

17 *"I've really been looking forward to today. After all the years I've known him, [groom] has finally admitted that I am in fact the best man."*

18 *"This is a very emotional day. Even I'm feeling a bit choked up. Mainly because I've had [groom's] hands around my neck, threatening to kill me if I mess up the speech.*

Everything's so emotional. Look, even the cake is in tiers."

19 *"While travelling here I was wondering, as best man, how much I could drink without anyone noticing... [slurring] And I think that I have badly misjudged it.."*

20 *"I'd like to start this speech by introducing myself. [Best man], being a clever old chap, decided to dispense with the speech-making part of his best man's duties, and has employed the services of our company to take over from him.*

Speeches R Us specialise in all those family occasions when a speech fits the bill: weddings, funerals, disciplining children in a patronising manner – you get the gist. Anyway, we deliver a personally tailored speech for every occasion. Ask me afterwards for a brochure..."

21 *"I couldn't help noticing that there's a bet on about the length of the best man's speech. Well, just to let you know, there might be a bit of insider dealing afoot. I placed a bet of an hour and a half. With the kitty currently at about £200 you might as well all settle back, make yourselves comfortable and enjoy the ride..."*

22 *"When he asked me to be his best man, you know, organise a stag weekend, get him to the church on time, and say a few nice words at the reception, I told [groom] it was a great honour to be asked, but that, quite frankly, I felt he'd be better off with someone else.*

Then he offered me £50.

I said indignantly: "I'm not a man who can be bought!"

Then he offered me a £100....

Anyway, good afternoon, ladies and gentlemen. My name is [best man] and it's my pleasure to be [groom's] best man today."

✧ SUBJECTS TO AVOID

There's nothing wrong with embarrassing the groom – he and all of the guests will expect you to do this – but you don't want to humiliate him. That's what the stag night was for. During the wedding speech you want your words to make him laugh and blush. Not cry and go green. If in doubt, leave it out.

DON'T MENTION ex-girlfriends. Everyone knows the groom has had past loves, but no one particularly wants to be reminded on his wedding day. Lurid tales of ex-paramours will just make the groom squirm in his seat. It will make the bride and both sets of parents extremely uncomfortable. And any ex-girlfriends who happen to be present among the guests (there's always one) will be mortified.

DON'T IMPLY that the groom is a womaniser. Even if he's spent all day with his hands all over the bridesmaids, don't even mention it. Have a stern word with him, yes. But don't tell everyone else.

DON'T MENTION divorce. One of the newly-weds may well be a divorcee. If they are then everyone will know. So don't bother reminding them. It will be seen to be in bad taste.

DON'T MENTION heavy drinking, drugs, gambling or fighting. These particular habits are very close to the bone. There will be other safer material about which you can mock the groom.

DON'T MENTION sexually-transmitted diseases.

NEVER MAKE FUN of the bride. This area is for the father of the bride's speech, not yours. Even if the groom has chosen someone you certainly wouldn't say was beautiful, as far as you're concerned, today she is a paragon of pulchritude. Don't ever forget that.

AVOID racist or homophobic jokes. They're not funny and you'll just end up looking like an idiot.

AVOID sexist jokes. A little light banter about how the groom might end up being hen-pecked by his new wife is okay. But anything stronger won't go down well. Remember that around half of your audience will be female.

DON'T MENTION arguments between the bride and groom. Even if they tend to fight like cat and dog, no one, least of all them, will want to be reminded on their wedding day. You're supposed to be celebrating the union between man and wife. Not disunion.

MOTHER-IN-LAW jokes are clichés. Think of something more original. Besides, if you mock her she will think the groom put you up to it.

DON'T MAKE FUN of the bride's friends. She may suspect you and the groom have a conspiracy against her. You'll also halve your chances of having a drink bought for you afterwards.

DON'T EMBARRASS either set of parents, however tempting it may be, and never make jokes about the ceremony or the reception. You can bet your bottom dollar that the whole day cost the bride's father an arm and a leg. Besides, you're eating and drinking for free.

DIRTY ADULT JOKES are a no-no. Seaside postcard humour is okay, but anything stronger will get a mixed reception.

DON'T TALK ABOUT the performance of either bride or groom in bed. In any case, how would you know?

DON'T MENTION unemployment if either bride or groom have recently lost their job. You want people to think they stand a chance of a happy life together, don't you?

DON'T MENTION any psychological counselling either newly-wed might have undergone. Very few receptions have leather couches to lie on.

DON'T BRING UP past brushes with the law. Even if the groom is an ex-convict, no one will want reminding. Least of all the father of the bride.

HOW RUDE CAN YOUR JOKES BE?

Don't assume that the grannies and grandpas at the wedding haven't heard rude jokes before. They were telling smutty stories before you were born. Having said that, the last thing you want to do, as best man, is offend anyone at the wedding. A light-hearted story about the wedding couple being caught in bed by the in-laws will amuse everyone, grannies included. But a graphic sexual description is pushing the envelope too far. You only have to hint at something sexual and everyone who is supposed to will know exactly what you mean. The only guests who won't are the underage ones and you don't want them to in any case. The golden rule is: if in doubt, leave it out.

The chief usher at my wedding has never forgotten a wedding he attended a few years ago. The parents of the bride were born-again Christians and were very proud to have secured the services of the local vicar who was delighted to be the one to marry the young couple.

After a very lengthy traditional Anglican service, everyone went straight from the church to the wedding reception which was being held, at great expense, at a stately manor house in the countryside. Once all the guests arrived, the receiving line was longer than a milkman's round. Best man and, as it happens, the vicar, were both dying for the toilet but quickly discovered there were no facilities until after they had queued up and been through the receiving line. Thinking no one would notice they both nipped around the side of the stately manor in the back garden. Fortunately no one spotted them.

When it came to the speeches, the best man thought he would regale all the guests, many of whom, like the bride's parents, were born-again Christians, with a story about how he and the vicar had been caught short together. When no one laughed he thought he'd go one step further and supply a few details about the size of the vicar's manhood. Well... if you thought the vicar was mortified, imagine what the bride's parents and their friends thought. The best man had misjudged the occasion. Some things are better left unsaid.

✦ SAFE JOKE MATERIAL

A best man's speech isn't complete until you make fun of the groom. It's difficult sometimes knowing what traits of his to mock. The following are generally considered safe territory: old school reports, lack of skill in the kitchen, lack of DIY skills, dress sense, table manners, poor physical fitness, vanity, slobbishness, singing skills, lack of culture, poor haircuts, embarrassing stories from childhood and school; driving test.

✧ IDEAS

People are expecting anecdotes and funny episodes about your relationship as best friend of the groom. Think back to when you first met the groom. Perhaps you were at school or college with him. Maybe you've both worked for the same company. You're bound to have played sport together, gone on holiday together and certainly gone out drinking together. All these adventures, however mundane, will provide a wealth of material.

You may even be able to include things that happened on the stag night (keep it clean); or you might add last minute details from earlier during the wedding day.

If you haven't known the groom for that long then why not quiz his family members beforehand for some funny episodes from his life? Ask about his childhood, his birthdays, his pets, his first car, family holidays, former jobs, etc. Old school friends will be able to throw up some great little stories. What about asking his parents for an old school report? Read that out during the speech and you're guaranteed to get some laughs.

A friend of mine was at a wedding in the USA where the bride's uncle was asked to make a speech. Somehow the crafty old fellow managed to get hold of a teacher's report from when the bride was at junior high school. When it came to reading out her English lesson report the guests were in hysterics as the uncle relayed the terrible things that the teacher had written about his niece's lingual incompetence. Not surprisingly the bride was mortified with embarrassment, but it wasn't until after he'd finished the speech and she'd told him that her old English teacher was in fact one of the guests that he realised just how embarrassed she really was.

Once you start thinking about times and experiences you have shared together you'll find that you're able to jot down loads of amusing yarns from the groom's past. The more embarrassing (within reason), the better. People laugh at things they can identify with. There's little point telling a story about something no one in the audience will be able to relate to. But if it's a genuine story that really happened and you think it's funny, then it probably will be funny for everyone else. The more details you include, the more genuine and therefore amusing it will seem. Then again, don't be afraid to embellish or exaggerate where you see fit.

Although it's the job of the father of the bride to tell stories about his daughter, you may want to include the odd anecdote about the bride and groom as a couple.

Your speech isn't just about taking the mickey out of the groom, however. You should think of some heartfelt and poignant material, too. Perhaps something that proves what a great friend and husband he is.

✧ QUOTATIONS

Many orators like to include a couple of choice quotations in their speech. Why not? As long as you don't use more than a couple and provided they are appropriate and you can link them into the speech, then they can make a worthy addition. They may even, if you're lucky, make you sound learned. A few examples follow on pages 96–102 and see pages 123–124 for sources of further quotes and poems.

Marriage

> *"Marriage is the highest state of friendship. If happy it lessens our cares by dividing them, at the same time that it doubles our pleasures by mutual participation."*
>
> Samuel Richardson

> *"Marriage is our last, best chance to grow up."*
>
> Joseph Barth

> *"'Marriage'. This I call the will that moves two to create the one which is more than those who created it."*
>
> Friedrich Nietzsche

> *"A princely marriage is the brilliant edition of a universal fact, and as such it rivets mankind."*
>
> Walter Bagehot

> *"A successful marriage is an edifice that must be rebuilt every day."*
>
> Andre Maurois

> *"All married couples should learn the art of battle as they should learn the art of making love. Good battle is objective and honest – never vicious or cruel. Good battle is healthy and constructive, and brings to a marriage the principle of equal partnership."*
>
> Ann Landers

"I used to believe that marriage would diminish me, reduce my options. That you had to be someone less to live with someone else when, of course, you have to be someone more."

Candice Bergen

"Marriage is the union of disparate elements. Male and female. Yin and yang. Proton and electron. What are we talking about here? Nothing less than the very tension that binds the universe. You see, when we look at marriage, people, we're looking at creation itself. 'I am the sky,' says the Hindu bridegroom to the bride. 'You are the earth. We are sky and earth united.... You are my husband. You are my wife. My feet shall run because of you. My feet shall dance because of you. My heart shall beat because of you. My eyes see because of you. My mind thinks because of you and I shall love because of you.'"

Diane Frolov and Andrew Schneider, *Northern Exposure*

"Marriage. It's a hard term to define. Especially for me – I've ducked it like root canal. Still there's no denying the fact that marriage ranks right up there with birth and death as one of the three biggies in the human safari. It's the only one, though, that we'll celebrate with a conscious awareness. Very few of you remember your arrival and even fewer of you will attend your own funeral."

Diane Frolov and Andrew Schneider, *Northern Exposure*

"Nearly all marriages, even happy ones, are mistakes: in the sense that almost certainly (in a more perfect world, or even with a little more care in this very imperfect one) both partners might be found more suitable mates. But the real soul-mate is the one you are actually married to."

J. R. R. Tolkien.

"Intimacy is what makes a marriage. Not a ceremony, not a piece of paper from the state."

Kathleen Norris

"A successful marriage requires falling in love many times, always with the same person."

Mignon McLaughlin

"That is what marriage really means: helping one another to reach the full status of being persons, responsible and autonomous beings who do not run away from life."

Paul Tournier

"A good marriage is one which allows for change and growth in the individuals and in the way they express their love."

Pearl Buck

"I love being married. It's so great to find that one special person you want to annoy for the rest of your life."

Rita Rudner

"Never marry but for love; but see that thou lovest what is lovely."

William Penn

"A good marriage is like a good trade: Each thinks he got the better deal."

Ivern

"After seven years of marriage, I'm sure of two things – first, never wallpaper together, and second, you'll need two bathrooms... both for her. The rest is a mystery, but a mystery I love to be involved in."

Dennis Miller

"An occasional lucky guess as to what makes a wife tick is the best a man can hope for. Even then, no sooner has he learned how to cope with the tick than she tocks."

Ogden Nash

"Chains do not hold a marriage together. It is threads, hundreds of tiny threads which sew people together through the years. That is what makes a marriage last – more than passion or even sex!"

Simone Signoret

"For it is mutual trust, even more than mutual interest that holds human associations together. Our friends seldom profit us but they make us feel safe... Marriage is a scheme to accomplish exactly that same end."

H. L. Mencken

"I would say that the surest measure of a man's or a woman's maturity is the harmony, style, joy and dignity he creates in his marriage, and the pleasure and inspiration he provides for his spouse."

Benjamin Spock

"Marriage is like a pair of shears. Oft times working in opposite directions, but punishing anyone that comes between them."

Sydney Smith

"The more you invest in a marriage, the more valuable it becomes."

Amy Grant

"In marriage, each partner is to be an encourager rather than a critic, a forgiver rather than a collector of hurts, an enabler rather than a reformer."

H. Norman Wright and Gary J. Oliver

"Car manufacturer's formula for a successful marriage: Stick to one model!"

Unknown

"I pay very little regard...to what a young person says on the subject of marriage. If they profess a disinclination for it, I only set it down that they haven't seen the right person yet."

Jane Austen

"Marriage – as its veterans know well – is the continuous process of getting used to things you hadn't expected."

Tom Mullen

Love

"*Love is the immortal flow of energy that nourishes, extends and preserves. Its eternal goal is life.*"

Smiley Blanton

"*A relationship is like a rose,*
How long it lasts, no one knows;
Love can erase an awful past,
Love can be yours, you'll see at last;
To feel that love, it makes you sigh,
To have it leave, you'd rather die;
You hope you've found that special rose,
'Cause you love and care for the one you chose."

Rob Cella

"*All thoughts, all passions, all delights.*
Whatever stirs this mortal frame.
All are but ministers of love
And feed His sacred flame."

Samuel Taylor Coleridge

"*Woe to the man whose heart has not learned while young to hope, to love – and to put its trust in life.*"

Joseph Conrad

"*We are all born for love. It is the principle of existence, and its only end.*"

Benjamin Disraeli

"*You will find as you look back upon your life that the moments when you have truly lived are the moments when you have done things in the spirit of love.*"

Henry Drummond

"*Immature love says: 'I love you because I need you.' Mature love says: 'I need you because I love you.'*"

Erich Fromm

"In love the paradox occurs that two beings become one and yet remain two."

Erich Fromm

"The moment you have in your heart this extraordinary thing called love and feel the depth, the delight, the ecstasy of it, you will discover that for you the world is transformed."

J. Krishnamurti

"Treasure the love you receive above all. It will survive long after your good health has vanished."

Og Mandino

"To love deeply in one direction makes us more loving in all others."

Anne-Sophie Swetchine

"Perhaps the feelings that we experience when we are in love represent a normal state. Being in love shows a person who he should be."

Anton Chekhov

"The meeting of two personalities is like the contact of two chemical substances: if there is any reaction, both are transformed."

Carl Jung

"To love and be loved is to feel the sun from both sides."

David Viscott

"All love that has not friendship for its base, is like a mansion built upon sand."

Ella Wheeler Wilcox

"Love is everything it's cracked up to be…It really is worth fighting for, being brave for, risking everything for."

Erica Jong

"There is always some madness in love. But there is also always some reason in madness."

Friedrich Nietzsche

"What else is love but understanding and rejoicing in the fact that another person lives, acts, and experiences otherwise than we do...?"

Friedrich Nietzsche

"There is no remedy for love but to love more."

Henry David Thoreau

"Love is the difficult realization that something other than oneself is real."

Iris Murdoch

"Age does not protect you from love. But love, to some extent, protects you from age."

Jeanne Moreau

"To love is to receive a glimpse of heaven."

Karen Sunde

"Love is an exploding cigar we willingly smoke."

Lynda Barry

"Real love is a permanently self-enlarging experience."

M. Scott Peck

"To be brave is to love someone unconditionally, without expecting anything in return. To just give. That takes courage, because we don't want to fall on our faces or leave ourselves open to hurt."

Madonna

"Love is an act of endless forgiveness, a tender look which becomes a habit."

Peter Ustinov

"For one human being to love another; that is perhaps the most difficult of all our tasks, the ultimate, the last test and proof, the work for which all other work is but preparation."

Rainer Maria Rilke

"He who is in love is wise and is becoming wiser, sees newly every time he looks at the object beloved, drawing from it with his eyes and his mind those virtues which it possesses."

Ralph Waldo Emerson

"One word frees us of all the weight and pain of life: That word is love."

Sophocles

✧ THE TOAST

In theory, the best man is not officially expected to make a toast at the end of his speech. The father of the bride will have toasted the happy couple and the groom will have toasted the bridesmaids.

But in practice, if you want to toast the bride and groom again at the end of your speech, then why not?

The toast should always come at the very end. So as not to spring it on the guests unawares, always give them a few moments' notice to charge their glasses before you raise your own. You should have put aside a glass of bubbly near you at the beginning of your speech in readiness. Once everyone has had a chance to refill theirs, raise your glass in the air and propose a toast. Below are a few toast suggestions. Always finish off the toast with the words: *"To the bride and groom."*

> *"My greatest wish for the two of you is that through the years your love for each other will grow so much that years from now you will look back on this day, your wedding day, as the day you loved each other the least."*

> *"May the best day of your past be the worst day of your future."*

> *"Here's to the groom, a man who keeps his head though he loses his heart."*

> *"May the roof above you never fall in and may you both never fall out."*

> *"To the lamp of love — may it burn brightest in the darkest hours and never flicker in the winds of trial."*

> *"May 'for better or worse' be far better than worse."*

> *"The man or woman you really love will never grow old to you. Through the wrinkles of time, through the bowed frame of years, you will always see the dear face and feel the warm heart union of your eternal love."*

> *"May you have many children and may they grow mature in taste and healthy in colour and as sought after as the contents of the glass."*

"Let us toast the health of the bride. Let us toast the health of the groom. Let us toast the person that tied. Let us toast every guest in the room."

"Happy marriages begin when we marry the one we love, and they blossom when we love the one we married."

"There is nothing nobler or more admirable than when two people who see eye to eye keep house as man and wife, confounding their enemies and delighting their friends."

"Here's to the groom with bride so fair, and here's to the bride with groom so rare."

"Coming together is a beginning; keeping together is progress; working together is success."

"Seek a happy marriage with wholeness of heart, but do not expect to reach the promised land without going through some wilderness together."

CHAPTER 10

SPEECH DELIVERY

The manner in which you deliver your speech is just as important as the content. Take time to watch presenters or newsreaders on television. Think how great orators and stand-up comics perform to their audiences. They all deliver their words in different ways, but there's one thing they all share: stage presence. Those with the greatest stage presence are probably born with it. But it is a skill you can learn, too. The following tips will imbue even the most jittery of public performers with the confidence required. Armed with the right technique, even a nervous wreck can pass off as something of a rhetorician.

✦ PRACTISING

All the best speeches are rehearsed several times. Whether you're a politician, a stand-up comic or a best man you need to practise, practise and practise. And then practise a bit more. This will help you appear confident and ensure that your words flow smoothly.

If you partially memorise your speech then you'll be able to use cue cards rather than a fully written script – which will of course appear and sound a lot better and will allow you to look up at the guests as you speak. It's important to engage your audience.

Once you have all your brilliant words down on paper, there are then several ways to rehearse your speech:

1 Film yourself with a camcorder. This will give you a picture perfect idea of how you might look on the day – you can even dress up in your suit if you want to make it really authentic. A friend of mine did this and said he was so impressed by how professional he looked that on the actual day he was fearless and his speech went like clockwork.

When you play back the film you should pay attention to your stance, enunciation, gestures, pace and overall delivery. Make notes on things to work on and see if you can improve on subsequent practice runs.

If you don't own a camcorder then borrow or hire one. (Even an audio recording is better than nothing.) I cannot stress how much you will gain in confidence each time you film yourself and see yourself improving.

2 Make your speech in front of a mirror. Again, if you like you can dress up in your suit and make your rehearsal realistic. Use a full-length mirror so you can analyse your gestures and stance. Since you'll be trying to watch your reflection, this technique will train you to look up towards the audience as much as possible.

3 Practise your speech in front of a close friend. Preferably choose someone who will give you an honest opinion and who isn't attending the wedding – otherwise they won't laugh at your jokes the second time round.

If they're not close to the wedding party they'll spot inappropriate material in the speech that you may have overlooked. An outsider's opinion on your delivery and presentation is very important too.

✧ DON'T GIVE IN TO NERVES

Every best man gets nervous about his speech. Even the most experienced and assured public speakers will admit that behind their confident exterior they are sometimes a complete bag of nerves. But a bit of anxiety is good. It is nature's way of making sure that we perform well under pressure. What you must try to do is transform your nervousness from negative energy into positive energy. With a lot of preparation and practise this is easily done.

First of all make sure you have run through your speech at least five times (see Practising pages 107–108.)

I have a friend who is regularly asked to make speeches at weddings and public engagements. He has a special method of preparation which may sound strange but is in fact extremely effective: he places his speech script in the bathroom and every time he goes in there he quickly reads it through. It doesn't take long before he knows his words inside out.

Before the wedding ceremony starts and everyone gets embroiled in their various duties, make sure you agree with the other speakers what order the speeches are to run in. Traditionally it's the father of the bride who kicks off proceedings. He is followed by the groom and then the best man. If you're nervous, the last thing you want to happen is that, during the reception dinner, just as you are tucking into your dessert, the father of the bride taps you on the shoulder and says: "Right, you're speaking in 30 seconds!"

Most wedding speeches take place at the end of the reception dinner. It's a good idea to pay a quick visit to the toilet five minutes before the speeches are due to start. You can check yourself in the mirror, remove any spinach from your teeth and ensure that you won't be desperate for the toilet by the time your turn comes. A best man, in particular, may have to wait up to 45 minutes for the father of the bride and the groom to finish their speeches before it's his turn to speak – you'd be considered very rude if you rushed off for a toilet break during their speeches.

For the vast majority of best men, the most nervous moment of their whole day is the few scary minutes just before they have to get up and speak. This is normally just as the groom is winding up his own speech. For the most nervous people it can feel like they're about to face an executioner. Take a few seconds to analyse the mood of the guests around you. They will be looking forward to your speech. They are on your side. They want you to do well and they want to laugh at your jokes. What can possibly go wrong? Even if you stumble over your lines, the guests will be polite enough to overlook it.

Many professional speakers perform a quick set of exercises just before they stand up to speak. In a wedding situation, as best man, you will perhaps be seated at the top table. You can't exactly step outside the reception venue during the groom's speech to ready yourself, but there are a few relaxation exercises you can do in your seat to get your mind and body ready for your big moment.

Sit upright with your arms by your sides and your feet flat on the floor. Take a deep breath through your nose and at the same time clench your fists, push your feet onto the ground and hunch up your shoulders. (Everyone will be looking at the groom at this stage, so don't worry too much what you look like.) Hold your position for a few seconds and then slowly breathe out while loosening your shoulders, fists and feet. Feel all your nervousness and stress evaporate. Continue breathing slowly and deeply until it's your turn to stand up and speak.

Just before you open your mouth for your great opening line, there's a psychological trick you can use to inspire yourself with confidence. Instead of pondering on your own nervousness, think instead about something happy or funny. Perhaps think back to the last great joke you told your friends down the pub, or a funny incident involving a member of your family. As you do this you won't be able to stop yourself from smiling, at least inwardly, and at the same time all your spirits will be lifted and the negative energy of your nervousness will disappear. Your face will relax, the guests will notice how comfortable you look and you'll be able to launch your speech with a confident and easy start.

These first few words are the trickiest bit. Once you've got through your introduction and made them laugh then, provided you've done your preparation, the rest of the speech should be plain sailing.

Don't be over-awed by the size of your audience. Believe it or not, there is actually a benefit to having a large number of guests: your jokes don't have to be that funny. If you only get a little titter from each guest, but there are 150 people present, then it will sound like loud laughing. You will hear this laughing and automatically be filled with confidence. Laughter is a great antidote for nerves.

It's so important to think positively about your speech in the hours running up to the reception. Believe in yourself and be confident that you are going to deliver a wonderful address. Don't dwell on negative aspects, but instead think about how the guests are going to enjoy and laugh at your words, and how proud of you the bride and groom are going to be. Again, it's a psychological trick, but it's true that if you are able to envisage your speech being successful and being received well, then it's highly likely it will be.

✧ DELIVERY AND PRESENTATION

Nervousness has a fairly unpleasant way of manifesting itself: shaky hands, dry mouth and sweaty palms and brow on the one hand and, in extreme cases, feelings of nausea and loss of consciousness. Fortunately most of these physical signs (bar the last one) won't even be noticed by most of the guests. In any case, there are certain things you can do to hide them. Shaky hands are a lot less noticeable if you use cue cards rather than large sheets of paper which will flap about. If you think you might suffer from dry mouth, then keep a glass of water near you during your speech and sip from it regularly. To avoid stammering, speak slowly and methodically – your speech will sound much better at this pace anyway. While a hot summer's day is perfect for a wedding, it's not ideal for a speaker who has to stand up in front of 150 people in a heavy formal suit. Just before you get up to make your speech, mop your brow with a handkerchief. Once you've got through the first few lines of your speech and everything is going well, your nervousness will disappear anyway and hopefully so will your perspiration.

Engage your audience

Try to get the guests on your side from the very start. This isn't difficult to do since they all want you to perform well anyway. As you stand up to speak, try to pick out three friendly faces in the crowd – one on the left, one in the middle and one on the right. They can either be people you know or just guests who look friendly. Throughout your speech you can keep coming back to these faces. You'll find their smiles will help maintain your confidence.

Provided your jokes are vaguely funny you'll find it easy to get the audience on your side. Fortunately the best man is usually the third person to speak at a wedding, so the guests will already be well warmed up before it's your turn. Even if you feel your words aren't that funny, there are other sure-fire ways to get the guests on your side. Ask them questions which you know will elicit a positive response: "Doesn't the bride look absolutely gorgeous?"; "Isn't the groom the luckiest man in the world?"; "Isn't this the most wonderful wedding reception?" Even the most cynical of wedding guests will have to greet these questions with a rousing cheer. The more positive and vociferous their response, the more confident you will feel about the rest of your speech.

Another way to engage the guests is to include some of them in an interactive joke you play on the groom. An old favourite is the key trick. Before the wedding, buy 15 blank keys from a key cutter. At the start of the reception hand out the keys to various female guests. Tell each one to keep the key in her pocket during the speeches, but also make them promise to keep quiet about your little trick. During your speech announce something along the lines of the following: "The bride is well aware that her husband has had quite a few girlfriends over the years. Now that he is happily married she is willing to overlook any past romances. But she would be very grateful if any ex-girlfriends here would kindly hand her back keys they may still have to her husband's flat." At this point all 15 of the women should walk up to the bride and groom's table, and with a sheepish "sorry" hand her key to the bride. The stunt is even funnier if you can get some heavily pregnant women or even a granny to participate too.

Pace and projection

Many speakers, especially the nervous ones, have a tendency to rush through their speech, as if it's an ordeal they want to get through as quickly as possible. Remember that a slow, deliberate address sounds far better than a hurried one. You should practise speaking slowly and clearly. If you listen to professional speakers you'll notice that they leave gaps between their sentences and pause before and after crucial phrases. It makes the words sound more heartfelt. Speak too rapidly and the guests may miss some of your choice words.

You don't have to shout, especially if you have a microphone. But you do have to enunciate each word and try to project it to the very back of the room or marquee. You can achieve this by articulating your mouth more than you normally would and by not tailing off at the end of your sentences. Imagine that you are speaking just for the benefit of the guests sitting at the very back of the room. Whenever I speak publicly, near the beginning of my speech I always check by picking out a group at the back and asking them if they can hear properly. If they can then you can rest assured that everyone else can too.

How to use a mic
Acquaint yourself fully with how the microphone works before you use it. At the beginning of the wedding reception it's a good idea to approach whoever is in charge of the sound (normally the DJ) and get them to show you how to adjust the stand and

switch the device on. You don't want to be one of those poor speakers who finds himself tapping the head of the microphone and looking around cluelessly asking "is this thing turned on?" It's never a great way to start any speech.

However confident you are in the strength of your speaking voice, don't decline to use a microphone if one's available. Even very strong speakers tend to tail away at the end of sentences. A mic will ensure that older guests with hearing aids (there's always at least one) and those at the very back hear every word you say.

I was at the wedding of one of my best friends recently where the microphone kept playing up. Every few minutes it would screech with feedback. Two of the speakers chose to use it, nonetheless, while the best man decided to give it a miss. But the reception was in a large hall and there was noisy traffic passing by outside, so even with all the feedback, the amplified speeches were much better received than the non-amplified one. Guests at the back of the room barely heard a word the best man said.

For maximum effect, your mouth should be about 20 centimetres (9 inches) away from the mic when you speak into it – that's just longer than the distance between your little finger and your thumb when you stretch out your hand. If you don't have a microphone stand, but just a hand-held mic, try not to wave it around as you speak or much of what you say will be lost.

Stance

The way you stand will have a massive effect on how you deliver your speech and how well it is received. For the guests, your stance will be the most obvious part of your body language. Try to stand upright with your arms down by your sides and your palms open to the audience. This will give the impression that you are confident, open and friendly. Avoid crossing your arms – which looks defensive – and keep your hands out of your pockets – which looks too casual. Place your feet shoulder-width apart with one foot very slightly in front of the other. Shift your bodyweight slightly forward so that you are on the balls of your feet. This will give your speech much more vigour than if you stand back on your heels.

If the microphone is on a stand, place it slightly to the side of your body so that you don't look like you're hiding behind it. And don't lean on it.

Avoid making a speech from behind a table. Try to move so that there are no obstacles between you and your audience. Some reception venues and marquees can be fairly cramped. You may find that speaking from behind a table is your only option. If this is the case then whatever you do, don't lean on the table – it looks aggressive and will put off the guests.

You could always move to another vantage point halfway through your speech. Some guests may not have an ideal view, or there may be pillars in the way. There's nothing to stop you facing one way for the first half of the speech and then moving your position slightly for the second half.

I remember a huge wedding I attended in France a few years ago. At the reception there were so many guests that when they sat down to dinner they filled two separate rooms. Fortunately people sitting in the smaller room were able to follow the speakers via a video link. But at one point the best man, using a portable microphone, walked from the first room and spoke for a while directly to the guests in the second room. He looked very confident and all the guests appreciated the extra effort.

Notes and cue cards

A lot of orators choose to write their speech out verbatim on a script. If you're not a very confident speaker then this is probably a good idea, but it looks much more professional if you try to memorize most of your words and then put key phrases on small cue cards. Sheets of paper tend to flap around while you're speaking, especially if nerves have rendered your hands a bit shaky. Cue cards, on the other hand, are much less flimsy. Ideally you want to be able to lift your head so that you're looking at your audience as much as you can. Reading verbatim won't allow you to do this, but occasionally referring to cue cards as prompting devices will (see page 86).

I remember watching a film of the first speech I ever made. Because I hadn't bothered to learn my words at all, I was forced to read it out from a sheet of paper word for word. It turned out that I only looked up at my audience three times during the whole speech – once at the beginning, once after I got a particularly loud laugh in the middle, and once at the end. The rest of the time I had my face buried in my script which looked awful. Even if you do have to read out your speech word for word, pause and look up at the guests as often as you can without losing your place. It makes such a noticeable difference.

Gestures/movements

No one wants to hear a speech delivered by a motionless waxwork dummy. But at the same time it can be very irritating if the speaker moves around and waves his arms about. You want to be animated but controlled.

A lot of nervous public speakers have annoying little habits they are completely unaware of. They jiggle coins in their pocket, they play with their hair, they cover their mouth, they sway from side to side, they rustle their notes, shuffle their feet, play with jewellery.

At first it may be endearing, but after a short while your listeners will find it irritating. If you get a chance to film your speech during practice you may be able to eliminate these movements and gestures.

Props

The right props can work wonders, while the wrong ones can be a disaster. Years ago I went to a beautiful church wedding where the family of both the groom and the bride were very religious indeed. The bride's parents were especially pious – so much so that as far as they knew their daughter hadn't yet shared a bed with the groom.

The best man, bless him, thought he would regale the guests with a bit of light-hearted banter about pre-marital sex. Halfway through the speech he produced a sports bag from under the table and proceeded to remove several (what he thought were amusing) props to illustrate his story. Imagine the bride and groom's horror when he brandished a set of handcuffs, a packet of condoms and a couple of pornographic magazines. Instead of the guffaws of laughter that the best man was expecting, there was stunned silence. The props immediately went straight back in the bag and the best man quickly and sheepishly hurried through to the end of his speech.

In order to achieve the desired effect the props have to be the correct props. I've seen speeches where the best man has used a projector to display photos of the groom when he was a baby. I've seen speeches where the father of the bride has revealed a security blanket that the bride had been inseparable from when she was a toddler. I've seen speeches where the best man has played a recording of the groom singing a solo on a drunken night out. All three occasions were received with good humour.

Think long and hard about the props before you incorporate them into your speech. And always remember: electrical props like CD players and projectors can, and often do, malfunction or go missing.

Be conversational

Just because you've spent weeks working out the funny and heartfelt words you plan to use in your speech, this doesn't mean that you need to deliver them in an especially formal or stilted manner. Try to be conversational. That's not to say that slang and swear words should litter your speech. Hopefully your words will be considered and imaginative, but the style that you deliver them in should be the same as the style of a normal, everyday conversation with a nod towards the formality of the occasion.

In times past wedding speeches were far more reserved and ceremonial than they are today. Granted, if you've been asked to speak at a state or royal wedding then your words should reflect the formality of the event. But at most of the weddings we mere mortals are invited to, we are among close friends. A certain respectful familiarity will be expected.

Try not to sound affected. Be relaxed and chatty when you speak. And don't put on airs and graces. If you have a strong regional accent then be yourself and use that accent to great affect. No one's expecting you to sound like the Queen. If you put on an act everyone will think you're being fake and insincere.

Years ago I attended a wedding in Oxford where the social backgrounds of the bride's and groom's family couldn't have been more dissimilar. The bride came from a very well-heeled, almost aristocratic family, while the groom was working class and proud of it. It turns out his best man wasn't so proud of it. You could tell that he had a strong Newcastle accent, yet he tried to disguise it by talking in a fake posh accent. No one was impressed, least of all the bride, and he ended up sounding like a buffoon.

Vocal variety - don't be monotonous

Even if the content is enthralling and witty, a speech delivered in the same dull, flat monotone can be the most excruciating thing to listen to. A bit of vocal variety will liven things up for the guests. Vary the pace, pitch and volume of your delivery in order to emphasise certain words. If you're quoting someone you may wish to impersonate their voice; speak louder at key moments and especially for the toast; some anecdotes may sound better if you recount them quickly, while others may benefit from a very slow delivery.

Next time you hear a speech listen to how the speaker varies the way he speaks. The more you're able to do this the more likely you are to keep your audience interested (and awake).

Dealing with interruptions/hecklers

Don't worry. You're not a stand-up comedian. If anyone interrupts your speech or heckles you it's probably just to encourage you or get a laugh. It can be very distracting, however, and put you off your stride. For the nervous speaker it can spell disaster. There are several failsafe ways to deal with interruptions. Don't get too involved with a heckler. Simply look across to them, nod in acknowledgement, say "Thank you very much for that" and carry on with your speech. You may even wish to acknowledge them by name (it's highly unlikely you'll get heckled by a complete stranger at a wedding) so that they get the attention they're obviously craving. Whatever you do, don't get into a debate with them otherwise you'll lose your train of thought and the whole momentum of the speech.

You may feel like defending yourself from a heckler and giving them some backchat, a bit like stand-up comics do. But remember, stand-up comics are quick-witted professional performers. If you, as an amateur, start trying to score points with a heckler it could backfire and get very uncomfortable indeed.

Above all, relax. Best men always tend to get too worked up about their speech. So what if you don't sound like a professional? So what if you don't make everyone split their sides with laughter? As long as you make an effort, sound sincere and engage your audience, everyone will love you.

USEFUL SOURCES

✧ WEBSITES

There are thousands of wedding and wedding-related websites out there covering every possible aspect of the big day.

General

www.bridesbook.net/

www.confetti.co.uk

www.hitched.co.uk

www.our-wedding-plans.co.uk

www.weddingguide.co.uk

Stag Celebrations

www.activepursuits.com

A one-stop directory for activities throughout the UK.

www.adventure001.com

Offer activities such as flying, driving, shooting and ballooning throughout the UK.

www.brilliantweekends.co.uk

Organise stag weekends throughout the UK and Europe.

www.chillisauce.co.uk

Offer stag nights and weekends throughout the UK .

www.clubclassbus.com

Pick up the stag party, queue jump into the best bars and nightclubs. Available in Edinburgh, Glasgow, Newcastle, London, Bristol and Manchester.

www.crocodileevents.co.uk

Organise stag weekends throughout the UK.

www.eclipseleisure.co.uk
Organise stag nights and weekends throughout the UK and Europe.

www.fantastic-days.com
Offer activities such as tank driving, archery, clay pigeon shooting and combat capers.

www.freedomltd.com/stagshome.asp
Offer day activities, stag nights and weekends, mainly in the UK.

www.greatescapades.co.uk
Stag weekends throughout the UK, and in Prague, Dublin, Amsterdam and Barcelona.

www.hotrocks.co.uk
Organise stag weekends in Nottingham, Cardiff, Bournemouth and Bristol.

www.itssorted.com
Offer stag nights, weekends – single and multi-activity.

www.lastminute.com
Although not a specialist 'stag' website, you can book travel, activities, sports tickets etc.

www.lastnightoffreedom.com
Offer stag weekends in UK and Europe, along with customised T-shirts etc.

www.maximise.co.uk
Activities and adventure sports and offer stag weekend packages.

www.murder-mystery-events.com
Murder mystery parties in a 'Carry On Agatha Christie style'. Offer stag night packages.

www.nationalkarting.co.uk
Lists indoor and outdoor karting circuits.

www.organize-events.co.uk
Offer stag weekends in the UK and Europe.

www.pt-yachtcharters.com/stag_hen.htm
Experience sailing or powerboating followed by a party night.

www.redsevenleisure.co.uk
Organise stag nights and weekends, both in the UK and abroad.

www.releasetravel.co.uk
Offer over 27 destinations in the UK and abroad for stag weekends.

www.stagweb.co.uk
Organise stag weekends, stag parties and stag nights.

www.stagweekends.co.uk
Stag weekend packages in the UK, plus Tallinn and Prague.

www.ultimatedayout.com
Organise activity days – sailing, power boats, racing cards and track days.

www.ukpsf.com
The United Kingdom Paintball Sports Federation – lists paintballing sites throughout the UK.

www.whackysports.com
Offer activity days for stag parties.

Limousine Hire

www.callalimo.co.uk
www.carsforstars-nationwide.co.uk
www.limohiredirectory.com
www.limoinlondon.co.uk
www.limoshop.co.uk
www.whatlimouk.com

Party Accessories/Fancy Dress

www.dressingupboxonline.co.uk
www.forevermemories.co.uk
www.noveltywear.co.uk
www.partybox.co.uk
www.partyforce.co.uk
www.partykingdom.co.uk
www.partystockroom.co.uk
www.staggerin.com
www.the-joke-shop.com
www.thepartyplacemailorder.co.uk
www.ukballoondecorators.com

Customised T-shirts

www.ac-design.org.uk
www.graphitee.com/stag_nights.html
www.t-shirtsonline.net
www.zikzak.co.uk

Wedding Car Decorations

www.confetti.co.uk/shopping
www.weddingwonderland.net/

Sources of Quotes for Speech

www.comedy-zone.net/guide/quotes.htm
www.famousquotes.me.uk
www.quotations.co.uk
www.quotationspage.com
www.whosaidwhat.co.uk

Speech Courses

www.instantspeakingsuccess.com
www.speakfirst.co.uk
www.professionalspeakers.org
www.public-speaking.org
www.school-for-champions.com/speaking
www.the-asc.org.uk

✧ BOOKS

De Vicq DeCumptich, Roberto; *Love Quotes* (HarperCollins Australia, 1996)

Lansky, Bruce (Editor); *For Better or for Worse: Best Quotes about Marriage* (Meadowbrook Press, 1995)

Metcalf, Fred (Compiler); Scully, Mike (Introduction); *The Penguin Dictionary of Modern Humorous Quotations* (Penguin Books, 2002)

Sherrin, Ned; *The Oxford Dictionary of Humorous Quotations* (Oxford University Press 2003

The Oxford Dictionary of Quotations (Oxford University Press 2004)

✧ ACKNOWLEDGEMENTS

www.quotationspage.com
www.worldweddingtraditions.com

INDEX